THE DAY GAUL DIED

BY PAT MIZELL

ACKNOWLEDGEMENTS

I've been a reader all my life. The first book I ever read was *Gone with the Wind* when I was eight years old. I can still see the shindigs at Tara and Twelve Oaks and smell Atlanta burning and watch that magnificent Rhett Butler strutting into a room with a Virginia Reel playing. Margaret Mitchell didn't just write a book, she brought a time to life. I saw it, I felt it, and I was in it. Since then, I've read books that I learned things from, and I've read books that entertained me. But the best books were always the ones that took me inside them. I've tried to do both with *The Day Gaul Died*.

History is so much a part of my life but can be so boring to many. I ask myself why. Is it because of the way it's presented? I think so. To understand history you have to put yourself there. You've got to feel the fleas biting you when you're on campaign, and gag at the dust that a column of soldiers puts out. And more importantly, you've got to know "why" and not just the "what." The way I've tried to do this is create a human story that leads you through an event.

I need to thank some people. First, Desmond Dinan, professor and friend at George Mason University for first suggesting that I should write. Then Bernard Cornwell who has entertained me to no end and for pointing out that "telling the tale" is the important thing. Before I wrote the first word, I contacted Simon Turney, whose books I had just read. My thought was that the guy on the other side of the wall hadn't had his story told. Simon's encouragement to tell the other side of the story got me started and kept me going.

Then I met Ron Peake who had just published his first book. Ron is the most confident guy I know, but in sharing the hopes and fears of a first book, I felt like we were just two kids sitting in the dark with our arms around each other. Ron introduced me to Marina Shipova who provided the beautiful artwork you see. Then we both met Beth Lynne who became my editor and designated ass kicker; or is that redundant? Here's my tale. I hope you enjoy it.

Pat Mizell

My name is Vercassivellaunus, or at least it was in the time of the story I'm going to tell you. I am of a people that came from a land far away; over the centuries, we crossed the mountains that separated the lands of the east from the lands of the west and made our way up the great river called the Danus. We spread from there to the south and into the peninsulas of Italia and Hispania and even across the water in the west to the isles of Britannia. But this is the story of those of us who lived in a land called Gaul. The ancient Greeks called us the Keltoi.

I am of a society as old as our people; we were called the druidae. Much has been said of us, and most of it is wrong. We weren't sorcerers or mystics, only men with the gift to understand the past and see the consequences of what could come. We were only there to guide; as I am now.

Much has been written about Gaul and Caesar, but not all; you need to know more than just what one man said. I'm here to tell you what I saw, only that. You decide the truth. But one thing to remember, my life's path as well as paths of others once seemed very clear and straight; I've learned that all of us sometimes turn the wrong way. Judge others with that thought.

This is the story of a man named Vercingetorix and that wonderful time when he united the people of Gaul to recapture their freedom. He was my friend.

~Vercassivellaunus

PAT MIZELL

PART I

THE BEGINNING

PAT MIZELL

I am bleeding from my shoulder and my back but that isn't my worry; my horse is wounded and shot, even worse than I am. My sixty thousand men had been met with a precision and fury from the Roman legions that destroyed them as a fighting unit and now I am riding for my life. The Roman cavalry had been after me all day and I knew that if I didn't make it to the mountains soon, they would have me. Reaching the foothills, I follow a shepherd's path higher and higher into the mountains, but I finally need to make a decision. If Epacos dies on me, the Romans would search until they found me; I have to do something now.

I make my way around a turn on a high and narrow trail then dismount and strap my helmet to the bloody saddle; I cover the horse's eyes with my tunic and lead him to the edge of the cliff and over to the rocks hundreds of feet below. When I look down, I see the stallion's body lying there with my helmet beside him. Then jumping from rock to rock so there would be no footprints, I make my way further and further up the mountain. I climb until there is no light to see by, then I use a little footpath that had seen other travelers and shepherds. Finally, I stop and build a fire underneath an outcropping of rock. Others have been made there before. I have to find some wood, but I can only warm myself for a while; I have to have a hiding place. I can't outrun the Roman cavalry.

Under a protruding rock, I find not only wood, but a small opening into the mountain. It is a fair cave with a narrow entrance. It's cold but I'm out of sight. I go back to my fire, put it out, cover it with dirt, and create a false trail leading onward up the footpath. Then after a while, I double back and crawl into my cave. Through the entrance now, I push up dirt and rocks from the inside leaving only a small air hole. I will hide there and wait for the Romans to pass and for my bleeding to stop. Maybe if they find the dead fire the next morning, they will continue to think I had gone over the cliff with Epacos and that is just a passing shepherd's fire. I will hide here for a few days. I am bleeding, but I have some bread, and water is trickling from a little crevice.

PAT MIZELL

CHAPTER I

We rode fast over the ridgeline and then into a full gallop when we saw the dogs entering the trees. Vercin went for one side and I went for the other. When the boar came out, we went for him. He didn't run far; big boars would rather fight than run and he came for me with his long tusks flashing. But my eight foot spear beat his six inch tusks and that day I won. It took some killing though. Vercingetorix slammed his spear into the animal as I had, but the boar's hide was tough and the animal went down fighting with the dogs all over him. We rode home that day side by side with the pig hanging from the spears that lay across our saddles. It was summer in Gaul; we were princes of the Arverni and this was what we lived for: the chase, the hunt, and the fight.

When we got back to my farm, Vercin's father was there, arguing with mine, the way that brothers do. They seemed almost to hate each other sometimes; not like Vercin and me. He and I were cousins but loved each other as brothers should and called each other such. But that night we were all family again and celebrated our hunt with beer and laughter all around, while we butchered and ate the giant boar. He was magnificent. Vercingetorix and I had many such wonderful days back then, before I left for the druidae. Before Caesar came.

* * * * *

I left that same year. My name is Vercassivellaunus and I am of the Arverni. The druidae chose me when I was young to go with them while Vercingetorix stayed for his rightful place to become king someday. Druidae was a way of life. They were the wise men of our culture who knew of things most don't. They taught me the history of our people, and of our world. We Arverni were only one of the scores of tribes of our people, but we were the kings of all, before the Romans came and weakened us.

11

The druidae came from the noble classes, selected at a young age by existing druidae for different reasons; the ability to gain knowledge was one, the ability to do much more than that was another. Our training never ended, for there was much to learn about and from the past and we had to know those things so we could guide our people. There were stages in our development and for the first few years, I learned of those who had lived before us. Our masters knew of these things and applied this knowledge to lead our people in the present. Some of them, like my mentor Draius, could see more than the past.

The druidae were amongst the world from the beginning. The Greeks were the first who wrote of us, but then they were the first to look beyond their world. We were already there. We didn't write our histories down; we druidae only trust another to tell things as they were. It's too easy for the written word to be corrupted.

In the Keltic society, like all others, there are different classes. All of our people are equal in the eyes of each of us, but some have different talents and different ambitions and over the generations, these determine the rich from the poor and the warrior from the craftsman and the farmer from the merchant. The leadership, of course, comes from the prosperous. All Kelts are warriors at heart, even us druidae, but we were not expected to fight or farm or have to do anything that detracted from our role.

We are the judges, the historians, the religious leaders, the ambassadors, and the advisors to our people. We are picked for special talents; as boys, we have to show the ability to learn and understand the past; for we will be advising our people based on that knowledge and ability. Some of us show signs of powers that are far beyond these. I could see the future. Not clearly yet, but often. My master, Draius, said that my power would develop as I aged and experienced the realities of the world.

It took years and years of training for a druida to train for his place in our tribes. The rites of our religion were led by druidae. Our religion was our love of nature and the order that the spirits of nature had placed on the earth. Our laws were fixed around these beliefs to keep the harmony that nature intended for us.

That meant that a druida was a judge also. When a person broke the laws and upset this harmony, we sacrificed them back to nature by fire.

A Keltic chief or king wasn't allowed to leave our tribal boundaries. If he did, that was a declaration of war to the tribe in which he traveled. However, the druidae could represent a tribe to another and he was allowed to travel freely. In the freedom to do so, we learned more about the world around us and the ways of others. Although druidae were members of particular tribes, we worked together across those boundaries to help stabilize our relationships with each other and the outsiders.

We had special places called Nemetos that were sacred. These were where we met and where we looked to nature for guidance. None of us lived in one, but often close by. In my case, I lived with my master and mentor Draius on his farm. For many years, I lived there and received my training. As you will see, that suddenly changed one day, but now I need to tell you of my people, the Keltoi.

* * * * *

The Greeks called us the "Keltoi." Our people came from the east long ago and migrated west along the river they called the Danus until we came to the Alpines. From there we spread into the lands of the Etruscans and the peninsula of Hispania, and even into the isles of Britannia; but most of us lived in the great lands about and west of the great mountains: the land called Gaul. Some of us developed different beliefs about things and followed different leaders, but we were all Keltoi. We didn't look like the people of the south. We were taller and fairer skinned than they were, but we weren't of the Germani either. Of Gaul, there was Aquitania and Belgae and us; but we were all one Gaul. The tribes of Germani pushed against us from the north, the Romans from our south, and later from within us.

* * * * *

Seven years went by before I went home from my druidae life. It was Vercingetorix's wedding summer. Draius had gone to the islands of Britannica to meet with other druidae, for word had come of the Helvetii. I suppose Draius thought I was druidae enough now that I wouldn't go back to the other ways.

13

Ladia was his choice for his wife. She was a beautiful girl and loved Vercin so, but then we all did. He was that kind of man. We had known her all our lives. The families came; we hunted, laughed, and feasted just like in the days of our youth. Vercin's farm was large and verdant; the woods were full of the boar and the deer that we lived to hunt. That summer Vercin would put his slaves to work in the fields and then we would go riding; sometimes on the hunt, sometimes just for the joy of the wind in our faces. We talked of my life with the druidae. Most people didn't talk about that much but there were really no secrets, except for the religious part. We were the keepers of knowledge. We were the ones that the people turned to for advice and we talked to the gods. But that's another matter. We mainly just spoke of my life there.

We hunted a stag one day, not an easy thing to do. We had taken a stand at the edge of the forest. Two of Vercin's slaves and his dogs drove the woods and the stag came to us. Then it was easy; both of our lances struck him at once. We feasted that night, all of us, on roasted deer and Vercin's grain and turnips with delicious fruit from his orchards, and lots of his father's wine; his Roman wine, the only thing from there we liked, including the people. We made music and Ladia danced, even though she was beginning to get a round to her belly; I think it was something more than the food in there.

Celtillus, Vercin's father, talked a lot of our way of life and the threats to it. "The Germani tribes want our land; but that is the natural order of the world, so we'll fight them and kill them any time they cross their river. Our land is for the Keltoi; we can live beside the other tribes of Gaul even if those Aedui want to hold sway. Most of them won't fight us after all is said and done. But the Germani are different, they are savage. Even when we capture them and make them our slaves, we have to watch them every day, or they go back to their wild ways. As for the other outsiders, the Greeks are happy where they live; they just want to trade with us, but the Romans want our land, and to make vassals of us. Even the Greek port Massilia has been absorbed by the Romans and is now a Roman dominion. We have no choice but to trade through the Romans, now that the Venetii of the western sea are under their yoke too. Our grains, our iron, our salt, our meat, must be sold to the Romans at Roman prices. Some of us, like my brother and your father, my druidae nephew, profit. Those few do while most of us toil under the Roman thumb. I don't know where it will all lead us, but I know I don't like any man telling me what to do and where I can go to sell my products."

Others felt the same way; we spoke about this as we roamed that summer. Life was bountiful and the land was kind to us, as were the gods. There was an undercurrent in it all; and our fathers argued just as all of Gaul argued as to what our course should be. Vercingetorix's father, Celtillus, and mine had grown up on this land but mine had left to become a merchant. He was a very prosperous merchant who didn't want a war. "I don't like to be told to whom and at what price to sell my grain and cattle," erupted Uncle Celtillus one night.

"No, said my father, "yet you like that glass of wine in your hand, the wine that came from Rome."

"I could drink Greek wine if Rome was gone, and more of it at cheaper prices," spat back Celtillus.

My father and the men like him were wealthy because of Rome, and didn't want to change things. Much less go to war with Rome. The massacre of the Helvetii had Gaul screaming.

* * * * *

Vercin rode back with me when Draius returned from the isles. Celtillus and Vercin wanted to know what the druidae thought about that massacre and what we should do in return. Romans should die.

Draius told him, "Rome is not the place it once was, Vercingetorix. It's not even a place anymore, but a way of life. Their legions have conquered the Greek lands, and those of the Hispaniola, and even Africa. Carthage was the last challenge to them. The druidae in Britannia know they will be there some day, after they finish with us. Rome is not the little city fighting for its freedom like it once was. Its armies are not their farmers defending their land. The aristocracy of Rome has grown rich off the spoils of their conquests and they want more. The armies give this to them, and in return they have to give to their armies.

The walls of Rome are bursting with people who demand bread and land. It appears that what we grow and produce is not enough for them any longer; they want everything we have. Tell your father that the Romans must leave, Vercingetorix. Tell him the druidae think that." Vercin went back; back to the arguments and the talk of blood and I resumed my studies. Then one day that all ended. And it all began.

* * * * *

Celtillus had been murdered. They said it was because he wanted to be king of all the Gauls, but I think it was because there were others who wanted to be king. He was trying to unite the Gauls and fight Rome and some didn't want that to happen. I left the druidae that day for Vercingetorix; he would need me now and Gaul would need him. My place was with Vercingetorix and his place was as our king.

After Celtillus was killed, the old men of the Arverni forced Vercingetorix away. They knew he thought the same way as his father did and they wanted things to stay as they were with their Roman friends. My father was part of that group; I knew he had no part of killing his brother but he did go along with the rich nobles and merchants who wanted to keep their power and influence. Vercingetorix must be our king.

Ladia and his children were with him, and I took them into my arms. Then I went to put on the deerskin breeches and the tunic that Ladia left for me, and Vercin came in with his jewelry. I put a shining copper torc around my neck and silver warrior bands on my arms. Then we rode to my father's farm to get something I had left there years ago; what I wanted most...my sword. It was like all our swords, heavy and as long as from my chin to my knees. It would be my way of life now. There were armor and a helm, and Vercin and I burnished them until they reflected the sun. I was an Arverni warrior again.

We buried Celtillus properly, as would befit an Arverni king. Friends came, tribal leaders came, and even some of the Roman merchants came to pay their respects. Celtillus came from kings and he would leave us as one; he would need things for his next life. Vercingetorix had his slaves dig the tomb on top of the largest hill on his farm so Celtillus would be able to see the ancient kingdom of his fathers, the kingdom that should now belong to his son. In it, we placed a vat of the finest Roman wine, his sword and shield, along with grain and other foods, and a pot of beer for his journey. He could be traveling a long way and a long time to his new life. Vercin and I dressed him in his finest tunic and breeches, with his armor of course, and armbands from each of his warrior relatives. His great golden torc was burnished until it shone, and then we laid him down and sent him away.

He received one last present, from a stranger. A man of the Venetii called Gerromir had ridden in as we laid our king in his grave. He had two Roman helmets hanging from his saddle, with a Roman head in each. Celtillus would have been pleased. It was a wonderful burial. The feasting and the drinking lasted for three days; and the plotting a few more. Men were there that we could trust. We had plans to make.

Vercingetorix and I took Ladia and their boys with us. We rode into the hills and camped beside a stream that flowed among them. The sun was warm on our faces and our love for each other surrounded us; we knew our life would change soon, but for the now, we would enjoy each other. We hunted and taught the boys the way of an Arverni man. We showed them how to stalk the deer and then what had to be done after the deer was killed.

"Killing a deer is easy my sons, it's the part before that where skill is required. They must be found and stalked, and afterwards it's very messy." Vercin was laughing as we showed the boys how to skin the doe. "You take your knife and cut between these two bones; here and here in both back legs below that joint. Then you push a cord or vine through them and hang the deer from a tree limb. Then the real fun begins." I was smiling at my nephews because I knew what was coming next. We hung the deer and made the incision. Then we started cutting the skin away. "It's important to keep the hide in one piece. If you hack it all up then you've wasted some of it. This is what we make clothes and boots from, and the vests that men wear when we go into battle."

"But, Father," said little Celtillus, "yours is metal!"

"Yes it is son, as is that of your uncle, but some men don't have iron vests and wear leather instead. It's not as protective, but better than nothing when a Roman sword is slashing at you."

"This deer stinks, Father." The little ones liked the killing part but the stalk was beyond them yet and the skinning and cutting was not a pleasant thing.

"I know son, but this is why you kill the deer and it must be done. Fresh blood and gore smells bad, from a beast or a man."

We rode the valleys and the hillsides with the joy and happiness of the children beside us. It was a leisure that would be a luxury in the days to come, and the beautiful Ladia made it a joy for all of us. While the boys played in the meadow nearby one afternoon, she washed and combed our hair. After it dried, she put it into the braids that we Arverni liked when we weren't at war. Our great moustaches and long hair were the mark of a Keltoi warrior. Ladia could make a man feel like a king. When we returned after a few days, we were all tanned and our hair was streaked by the sun and we rode the lands of our fathers as Arverni warriors should ride, as our own kings. Then we went home; we had matters to attend to.

First, we went to see my father. My father, Gobanitio, was not a hateful man, just a greedy and treacherous one. "I had no part of your father's death, Vercingetorix; I want you to know that."

"I know that, uncle, and I know who did. But will you continue to oppose me? That is my question to you. You need to think about that."

The answer to that was never clear, but other things were. Draius had sent me word, in the language that the druidae knew, of who was behind the assassination. His message was very clear: rid the earth of the men who had done this and the Aedui druidae who had directed it. We did.

Gerromir went with us. He was good at the thing we were going to do. We rode north to the home of the renegade druidae. He lived at the edge of a forest, of course. When he saw us riding up with the sun rising behind us, he knew why we were there. He tried running, but nobody was going to outrun Gerromir, especially an old man in a robe. There in that forest, we hung him from a tree limb and did what we had done to the deer; but the deer had been dead. When we rode away, we carried two things. One was his head.

We rode the countryside and gathered our friends and they rode and gathered theirs. Then we rode to Gergovia to claim Vercingetorix's crown. It wasn't easy; they resisted us. But something about men with swords can be very persuasive. My father and his friends stepped aside. We rode in and threw the druidae's head at their feet. Then Vercin took the other thing we had taken and showed it to them. "This is the hide of your friend; it's my battle pennant now. Do I need more of them for my war?"

It was our land now, and we would not be stepped on by them or the Romans, or anyone. Then we sent riders to the nearby tribes, and they to their neighbors. Then we started preparing. The right time would come, soon.

PAT MIZELL

The Romans passed by me this morning. I could hear them talking and arguing but finally they rode on. I am bleeding more and weak. If they don't come back, I'll look for food tomorrow, and maybe build a little fire tonight, but I will die here; I know that. At least I won't be taken to Rome in a cage like Vercingetorix. All is lost to me and my kinsmen now, but the Romans will remember us. My name is Vercassivellaunus and I fought by his side.

It's cold here in this cave, but I'm out of the wind. I spent the day cleaning my wounds and sitting by the air hole of my cave, listening for them; if they don't come back by dusk that'll mean they're not coming back this way, or at least not until tomorrow. I won't chance a fire; I can get through another night and day. Maybe the gods will favor me now; they didn't at Alesia. My people are destroyed; either dead or taken as slaves to Rome; and my kinsman Vercingetorix will be dragged through the streets of that hideous place on display for Caesar. But I won't see that; I'll either die here or somewhere killing Romans.

The Romans are back; I could hear them talking and could almost see them. Maybe they had followed the shepherd's path and were now coming back. They may have given up and now will go back to that cliff. If they climb now to Epacos's body I'm done for. They'll see it was a ruse and know that I am close by; but they'll have to look under a lot of rocks to find me. My fate depends on how much they want me; or what lies they may tell Caesar. Maybe they'll want their warm beds and our women more than they want me.

I've stopped bleeding. I scrape some moss off the cave walls and pack it in my cuts. But I'm very weak and hungry. I have a few crumbs of bread left and they must last me until the soldiers leave. Now they've started a fire, I can smell the smoke. It's getting dark; they must plan on spending the night here. They're cooking their food now, and laughing and probably drinking. It's torture for me to smell and imagine but it could be a good sign. Maybe they'll leave for their camps in the morning. I can outwait them.

CHAPTER II

The druidae had studied Caesar, as they had all the Roman leaders, and those of the Greeks and the Germani. They knew Caesar as an ambitious and ruthless man and that his soldiers would follow him anywhere he asked them to go. He came to his career as a soldier in Hispaniae, and then up the Roman path of ascendency until now he was governor of both Gauls; Transalpine above the mountains, and Cisalpine below. We knew that he wanted to make our lands a Roman province like the others were. The Roman people looked at their leaders for the glory and the new lands where their settlers could go. Caesar would give them ours; of that we were sure.

He probably wasn't any worse than any other man was; all men are guilty of the thirst for power and the foul deeds that come from that. He fed his men, he led them in battle, and he gave them the booty and slaves when they won. They won every time and they followed him. The Roman system made great soldiers and, often, great generals but sometimes a weakness appeared, and Caesar had his; he had to give Rome glory every day and every year.

Much has been said about Caesar; he was a great general. He would use that, and Gaul, as his stepping-stone to even greater power. Rome was a treacherous place; we had seen that. The rich men contended for power, just like everywhere, but Rome was worse than most. We had gone there, back before this all started, and listened to their thinly veiled lies; Caesar had that problem now.

It had begun seven years ago when the Helvetii left their homeland and started their migration to the land near us in Gaul. They had been living north of the large mountains for generations but the German tribes were pushing hard on them. Rome wouldn't help; they wanted the Helvetii to die for them there. When the tribesmen burned their farms and villages and started the move, the Romans attacked them, massacred them, and sent the remnants of the tribe back to their barren lands. Caesar had all kinds of excuses for his actions, but we knew what he wanted…he wanted our land and the lands of all the Gauls. So, the fighting began.

Rome and the Keltoi people had fought each other for years; we had invaded Rome and conquered it, once long ago. For a long time Rome had been content with ruling the part of Gaul south of the mountains, and trading with us on peaceful terms, even under tension most of the time. Then Caesar was appointed governor of our part of Gaul too. He had ambitions. When the Helvetii started their migration west, he used that for the excuse he needed to come in our land. He told the Roman Senate that he had to protect Rome's friends in Gaul. He warned the Helvetii to go home to their lands, and when they didn't, he destroyed them. Hundreds of thousands of people came west; the few that weren't killed or taken as slaves were sent back home to die for Rome when the Germani came. After they destroyed the Helvetii, Rome stayed.

When, a year later, the Belgae tribes revolted, Caesar destroyed them too, the way he always did; dividing them and setting one tribe against another, with promises made and privileges given. One of the Belgae tribes was picked by Caesar to control the others, for Rome. Then Commius, the great war chief of the Atrebates, started a war on Caesar. For a while, he was winning, but the Roman war machine was too powerful in the end. The Romans don't beat you with iron spears and iron swords; they beat you with their iron discipline. They listen to one chief, Caesar, while we tribal people have many with different thoughts about how to war. In the end, the Belgae fell because of that. Commius made his peace. Caesar was good at that; dividing the tribes with his favors and threats, for men are always greedy. For the next five years, any tribe that rebelled would meet the wrath of Rome; we could never win. We saw that, Vercingetorix and some others, like his father.

The coastal people met the same fate; Rome's navy was the reason for victory there. The Venetii knew that if they couldn't beat Rome on the sea they couldn't win, and they didn't. Every time Rome won a battle, they killed all the warriors and took the others as their slaves to sell in Rome or Massilia. That was why the Roman soldiers fought so hard, for the booty as well as the glory. We went to Rome, to no good. We saw what they were and what we would become.

During the next few months, our men moved quietly among our kinsmen in the other tribes. We knew who would be with us and who wouldn't. The Aquitani wouldn't, their great chief Adiatuanos had made that clear, but some of the Belgae might come, maybe. And the young men of the Aedui were forming among themselves, silently. The people knew something was going on, but there was always something going on; for five years now, Gaul had been seething. I'm sure Caesar sensed it too. He just didn't know from where or when it would come.

Gerromir the Venetii and I were staying at Vercin's farm. Some of the war leaders of other tribes came in. We talked about weapons and the tactics that the Romans used. One man, Brossix, a smith by trade, had served as an auxiliary in the Legions. He did their work for them, even had friends among them, but was never considered a part of them because he wasn't a Roman citizen. He knew how the Roman army worked. He had served in it for thirteen years before he left and came back to his tribe in Gaul.

Gerromir had been a seaman, like all the Venetii were, but when Caesar's navy had destroyed them and burned their city, he had been taken as a slave. He carried bags of grain on his back every hour of the day to put in their merchant ships on our rivers that took our goods to Rome. Then, at a lax moment, he escaped. He had planned well; he knew where the horses were and where he was going. He went to the mountains; he couldn't go home. There were others like him, men on the run. They moved about, heard things, and saw things. Some of them were hiding in order to live. Gerromir was there because he wanted to kill Romans. One day Gerromir came to us, with the two Roman heads to prove who and what he was.

Other leaders came and went; we talked and we planned. We made maps of the rivers and of where the fords were in them. We knew where the bridges and the Roman outposts were. We knew where Caesar kept his legions; they were scattered about, he couldn't feed them if he kept them all in one place. Vercingetorix knew how many of the Romans there were and how many men of the tribes we had to have. Every man of our tribes had a sword; it was our way of life. But not all had the armor and spears that the Romans did, nor their war machines, but we didn't plan on using those things anyway. We would fight with our hearts.

Vercingetorix and I went to the druidae. It was important to have them with us. Rome had been trying for years now to destroy them, for without their help we could not unite. Celtillus had known that and Vercin knew it too. The druidae had been discussing things among themselves for years now, and with their brothers in Britannia and the ones in the Roman provinces of Cisalpine Gaul.

We had to have the agreement of our wise men, for they knew our destiny. Draius, my old master, had wished me well when I left them; he knew how I felt and what I must do. He was there waiting when we came in.

"You have a gift, Vercingetorix; men follow you. The druidae have spoken to each other and to the gods. We even tried talking to the Romans, but their sweet words turn to vinegar too often. We must be our own peoples, not the slaves of Rome. So take your men and your swords and make them leave, it's our lands, not theirs. We went to Rome once, as ambassadors for all the Celts, even the ones in Britannia. They spoke of friendship and alliance, but afterwards, it was the same thing as we'd seen before. At the heart of it is that the Romans will never forget that our Gallic brothers conquered their city. Even if it was long ago, they still fear us and hate us. We have lived here forever, and always will. So, go and take it back for us. Remember this: we are a powerful people, but Rome has ways that we don't know. I've seen their cities, their roads, and their bridges. Don't take their might lightly, or Gaul will be destroyed.

"Raise up the tribes, the druidae are with you. I have looked into the future and you and Vercassivellaunus are not to die in this war. Many will, but not you. I can only offer you this wisdom: Vercassivellaunus is a druidae. He knows the ways and things that only we know. So listen to him and let him guide you. And then send him back to me when it's over."

The tribes started to come in, not all of them, but some. We were the Arverni and had always been kings; yet we needed others with us, particularly the Aedui. They were favored by Rome now and could not be trusted yet but there were those among them who felt like us. They wouldn't give their loyalty lightly, if at all. We had to have them with us if Gaul was to be united. The Belgae of the north had been beaten by Caesar and had the Germani about them; the Helvetii to the east had been destroyed, and the Aquitania wouldn't leave their mountains. Our neighbors, the Aedui, were left to make this war with us.

Gaul was quiet that year; Caesar had gone to the isles of Britannia to prepare his conquest there. He took Commius, the great war chief of the Belgae with him. Some of Commius' people had moved there long ago and they would help Caesar if Commius commanded them to. Commius was a ferocious warrior, but after the Belgae uprising, he had made his peace and in turn, his Atrebates had special status with Rome. We went about our preparations and our planning. Many of the tribes were with us now; the Aedui were still not declared but the young men there would join us when the time came.

* * * * *

Ladia was churning the milk. "Cassive, why aren't you with Vercin today? He's never without you anymore." Ladia was making cheese and butter and the boys and I were helping her. It was mainly me, but I was mostly just sitting around and eating bread with the new butter spread on it. The boys were running around the meadows and chasing cows and screaming most of the time. I liked being with Ladia, and the work was easy.

"He went to the Lemovices, and took Gerromir with him. Their chief is a man named Sedullos and he is very leery of our cause. Vercin wanted him to hear from Gerromir what Caesar did to his Venetii."

"Are you sure that Vercin just wanted you to be near me? Are you guarding me from Romans? My family is nearby and your men are too."

27

"There is no real reason, Ladia, I just told him what a good cheese man I am and needed to be here to guide you."

"Well, you are definitely good at spreading that warm butter on bread. Is it good?"

"Oh yes it is, and I can see Brossix missing with his hammer over there; that sword he's making will be round if he doesn't get some of it too."

She laughed, and when she did, the world was right. All of us loved her and our winter there on Vercin's farm. But we knew that men were dying all over Gaul; and that we would too some day soon. But not today or tomorrow. Vercin had asked me before he left to bring in some meat; there were many mouths to feed on the farm now. That night around our fire, me and the other men ate our soup and bread, drank the good beer that Vercin had made, and planned a hunt. We would take extra horses, saws, and axes and if our luck were good, we'd bring home venison and boar and the other creatures of the forest. Cernunnos, The Horned One, would provide.

We were gone for three days; and on our way home, we went by Draius' home to leave him some of our kill. The druidae didn't hunt, nor grow crops much, and many of us furnished them with what they needed; it was our way. In turn, they gave us their wisdom and guidance and talked to the gods for us; the Horned One told them how to lead us in this life and the next.

The men left but Draius wanted me to stay and talk. His wife made our meal from a fresh deer and we sat long into the night discussing Vercin's plans.

"All you're telling me is logical, Vercassivellaunus, but know that Caesar sees what you're doing and he'll take steps also. Don't let him draw you into his trap; you know how good he is at that. He'll attack you, tantalize you, and work one tribe against another. Are you sure of the Aedui?"

"Who knows in the end where they'll be, but most of them are with us now. The young men want the Romans gone too. I see your skepticism and I think Vercin knows this too. He never lets them go too long without involvement though; he doesn't want them to feel like they're not a part of us." It was troubling though, this union that we needed. For too long the Keltoi had gone their separate ways and listened to their own leaders and this plan was different for all of us. But Vercingetorix was a different man from most.

* * * * *

He came home. He rode in as a young god. His hair was flying, as we liked it when we were at war. Gerromir was with him, as was Sedullos, the king of the Lemovices. The Lemovices were with us now and Sedullos said he'd bring ten thousand warriors when the time came. Oh, the feasting and joyous night we had. We were all Gauls now.

Vercin called his leaders together; it was time to make some plans. He wanted everyone to know what we were up against and how we must prepare for this war. Brossix wasn't the only one who knew how the Roman army fought, but he knew the things that most of us didn't see when the fighting actually started.

Brossix told us of his years with them. "The Romans fight with their shields as much as they do their swords. When the Romans form a shield wall, each man will cover the one on his right with his shield. The shield has a metal center that protrudes like a snout. The Roman will use it to hit you if you come too close, or with his short gladius, he'll stab you from underneath it. When they form a wall there are lines of men behind the others, and if one falls another steps up to take his place. As the battle goes on and you're about to give out, the Centurions will give the wall men a rest with the line behind quickly moving through the front line and forming their own wall. The Roman tactic is like a battering ram; it just keeps pounding you and pounding you. When you lose your patience and react, then you lose the battle, and likely your life. You can't fight the Roman legions in the open once they've achieved their formation. And they can quickly change one to another. They are the best trained and best disciplined army the world has ever seen."

Vercingetorix listened to Brossix, as we all did that night. Brossix took pebbles and sticks and showed us on the ground how the Roman army was organized. "The basic unit is called the Contubernium. It has eight men; they share a tent and a cooking pot and there is a mule for each of these units that carry its supplies. Ten of these units make up the basic fighting group of the army; it's led by an experienced officer and is called a Century. The Centurion who leads this group is the heart and soul of the Roman army. He's not one of the pampered rich, but a tough man who's fought in wars and proved himself. In battle, he is at the front of the charge and the men follow him unquestionably. The Cohort is the main fighting force though; it has six Centuries and is about five hundred men. In turn, ten cohorts make a Legion. All in all, a Roman Legion is about five thousand men and six hundred mules plus spares and oxen to pull the carts; each Legion has four hundred cavalry plus the auxiliaries of subject nations that do the dying and dirty work for Rome. The Roman Legion is the might of Rome. It is led by a general that has the right to do anything, including life and death, and is completely self sufficient when at war."

"So how do we beat them?" asked one of our chiefs.

Vercingetorix and I went for a ride. We discussed all of these things; the powers and strengths of Rome and what we Gauls had as ours. He didn't want anyone else along, just him and me, so we didn't have the bragging and strutting that you get when fighting men get together. We had to have more than courage to win this war. The next day we told the men how.

"This is a sack of grain; it weighs almost three pounds. Every Roman soldier has to have this every day to live, so we'll take it away from them." Vercin and I had agreed on our tactics that day, on our ride, and had come back to tell the other men what we thought.

"They buy it from our merchants and they depend on our farms for their food. We are the farmers, which is our strength and their weakness. The Legions are far from their supply bases in Narbo and Massilia. If we can feed Rome then we can starve Rome. We cut them off from their supply of food; attack the boats that bring it from the Cisalpine, attack the supply caravans on the roads, and make the Legions chase us all around Gaul. We'll be all about them and the more they divide and pursue the less their power and the further they are from their supply bases. Brossix tells us that when a Cohort leaves their camp they carry the food they need for fifteen days. That's almost fifty pounds a man, plus his weapons and equipment. We'll run their asses all over Gaul. When they run out of grain, they starve.

"What we'll do is to begin storing our grain like we do now; but in places where they don't know of. We'll take the livestock into the woods and when their merchants come around, we'll tell them the crop is bad. We'll sell them enough to keep them dependent on us but not enough to give them reserves to march with. And when the time comes, we burn our fields and attack. Let them get into their formations, and stand there hungry. Then we'll ride circles around them and see how long they'll stay in Gaul." That was the way we saw it and that was the way it all began.

PAT MIZELL

I think they're gone. They left at dawn and it's been still all morning, except for the eagle above me screeching. I think there must be a nest up there. I'm weak and hungry. It's been three days since I've had anything but morsels of bread. What I would do for a bowl of beer and a roasted hare right now. But at least I'm alive.

I found the aerie; the eagle was on the nest. When he leaves at dawn, I'll get the eggs. I'll have food again. The Romans had left a few scraps of grain but I didn't eat them....I have another idea for them. I tore the hem of my tunic off and am fashioning a snare from it. Tonight I'll use it to try to catch a rabbit, but tomorrow I have something else in mind. I rigged a little noose on what I think is a rabbit run, and put a few nibbles of grain just out of reach beyond it...with a deadfall of a rock if the noose was nudged. The hunger is overpowering now but I've been patient for too long to let it overcome me. Just a few more hours now.

I caught no rabbit, but I did get two eggs from the nest. Sweeter than anything I've ever eaten. And I left another surprise for the eagle. I've got a noose in his nest, and I'm hidden close by. When he returns I'll spring my trap. The sun is hot but the wind cools me. I punched a hole in each egg and sucked them dry. Now I have something to put water in. That'll help while I wait. I just have to stay hidden and still.

I thought about that day a lot, that day Vercingetorix and I talked to Draius. Would I live? Does Vercingetorix in a Roman cage count as "living"? I got the eagle. At first, he just flew around his nest squealing and flapping his wings over the missing eggs. Finally, he alit, and I pulled my cord and we had a glorious fight, him and me. But I won, I had the sword. I made a fire that night, there in my cave and cooked him. If there were any Romans about, they couldn't see the fire or me; and if they smelled the smoke, they might just think it was their own. I think they're gone. I ate my bird, most of it, and now I'll sleep and make a plan tomorrow.

CHAPTER III

That last winter before Alesia, the tribes started the attacks. The Romans sometimes dispersed in the wintertime so they could feed their legions off the harvests of different tribes. That made them vulnerable. Caesar had gone to Britannia, with his eyes on another conquest. He thought we were subdued, but he found out differently. Then we found out what the fury of Rome could be like.

Seven thousand Roman soldiers were wintered in the land of the Eburones. They were not a powerful tribe; they tolerated the legions only because Caesar had lifted their taxes to the dominant ones nearby and now they had grain to spare, and sell to his army. The Romans paid well, but they reminded the Eburones every day who ruled them. The larger tribes nearby didn't like losing their vassal or their tribute in grain and they were mocking the Eburones. Then there was the Germani; always pressing and raiding and stealing and killing. Winter was always a hard time.

The Romans, under Sabinus, were enjoying their winter. No marching, no fighting; just plenty of eating and stout Gallic beer, and Eburone women. One day, a group of the young men attacked a group of soldiers who were gathering wood and they killed a few of them. Ambiorix, one of the Eburone chieftains, met with Sabinus and told him that this was just an outburst of young men's passion and not his tribe's feeling toward Rome. He explained that the young men were being ridiculed and stirred up by some of the other tribes, who were in fact themselves planning an attack on the Roman camp.

Ambiorix urged Sabinus to take his seven thousand men and go to a distant Roman camp. He told Sabinus that the Eburones continue to supply him with grain but it would be easier if the Roman soldiers were not there as a constant reminder of their dominance. Not all of the Roman officers wanted to do this; an officer named Cotta said it would be a violation of Caesar's orders, but Sabinus and the army marched out anyway. When they were on the road and spread out, Ambiorix attacked and slaughtered them.

Similar things happened all across Gaul; other northern tribes attacked Cicero and his Legions. They would have annihilated them but Caesar marched immediately from his quaters and saved Cicero and the Legions. The Roman Senate and Caesar's enemies within it criticized him and questioned his right to govern. The streets and halls of Rome were full of the talk of the Belgae uprising. Caesar knew that only blood would satisfy now; he knew how to furnish that.

Caesar took the wrath of Rome to the rebels. It was a dying time for Gaul, but only the shadow of what was yet to come. The group of us who now lived on Vercin's farm grew larger. We were his arms and legs and his eyes and ears. Each tribe had its own council of chieftains but we united Gaul. We worked out the requirements that each tribe was expected to meet: men, horses, swords, and food. We studied our maps and planned our assaults and ambushes, and the escape routes we would take. However, our people couldn't wait; a lot of them couldn't, and after the Roman retaliation against the north, the killing began again. Romans died and then Gauls died. That was the way it was.

Caesar then marched with ten legions and destroyed a people. The Eburones under Ambiorix fled to the Germani and were never a tribe again. That started a bloodbath all over the north of Gaul; Caesar didn't like to have his plans interrupted and the Belgae paid. We watched and waited. Then, Caesar made a mistake. He left Gaul.

* * * * *

After that bloody summer, Caesar went to his estate in the Cisalpine for the winter, leaving Titus Labienus in charge of his armies in Gaul. For some reason we'll never know, Labienus sent for Commius to come to a council and then tried to kill him. Commius escaped, though severely injured. That was the last time any Gaul ever trusted a Roman. Now the only one of the Belgae who was not Caesar's enemy became the fiercest one of all.

* * * * *

Decius Brutus and Gauis Delmonus met on the road leading to Caesar's villa; it was dawn, the time his staff always met.

"What is he cooking up today, Brutus? Will we invade Egypt, Persia, or Rome?" Delmonus joked.

Brutus laughed at that but not too much, for it was Caesar, after all. "I don't know, Gaius. Maybe he wants us to celebrate Bacchus with him tomorrow."

"I didn't know he ever celebrated anything," said Delmonus, "except maybe making us freeze our balls off in the middle of the night."

Caesar's generals gathered and then Caesar himself came into the room. Immaculate as always, with his customary smile, he said, "Thank you for interrupting your reverie. If it weren't important, I wouldn't drag you away from your beds and fires. So I'll get to the point. I want two Legions raised and trained and we start two days hence. I welcome your input on the how of it, but not the point itself. My decision has been made. We have options on who will be in charge of different aspects, so let's figure that out today. The sooner we can do that, the sooner you can resume the celebration of Bacchus tomorrow, and then we go to work. I want this army recruited, outfitted, and trained before the passes are open in the Alpines."

When the meeting broke up that afternoon, Caesar turned to a quiet man in the back of the room. "Stay a while, Caius, I have an assignment for you." Caius Spannus was not a general, nor even an officer, but he always attended when Caesar called a meeting. The generals all knew why; he was the one man Caesar would almost trust. "Caius, this is what I want you to do. Go to Massilia and Narbo and bring back any retired or disabled men who fought for me in Hispania. Get the pension roll from my clerk; he'll know where most of these men are. Take a Century with you and move fast. Tell my old men that Caesar needs them again; and to sweeten their love for me, tell them I'll pay a year's wages for six of their months. They can be home in time to plant, or whatever they do now. I have ten thousand raw recruits to train and I need men who can help me. Tell them they don't have to go to war with me, just prepare those who will.

Leave the day after tomorrow, Caius, and when you get to Massilia, find Asteraus and send him to me. I expect you know where to find him."

On the third day after this meeting, a man rode up to Caesar's estate. He was neither a young man nor terribly imposing in appearance, but he had skills that Caesar wanted. Spannus had found him where he always was, in his tavern on the waterfront of Massilia.

"Asteraus, you know men, and I trust you to do something special for me. Get a few who have ears and not running mouths. Get men who don't look like soldiers; get men who will fit into the crowd. I want you in Rome in a week's time and I want your men to mix in, listen, and find out what Rome is thinking. I know what the politicians and patricians think, but I want to know what the Roman people think. Are they with Caesar. Who do they hate, who do they love. Find out what they need and what they think they need. Scatter your men over the city, never meet together as a group, but you meet with each one every day. Find out the thoughts and feelings of Rome and be back here by the last day of Ianuarius. And Asteraus, one more thing, have you ever wished to kill a Roman general?" Caesar laughed as he turned and left the room, but Asteraus knew this wasn't just a casual remark. He had served Caesar before and Caesar paid well.

Asteraus and eight other men of his kind arrived at the outskirts of Rome, where they stabled their horses and then told the farrier they would be back in three weeks. After spending the night in a local inn, they, one by one, made their way into different areas of Rome. Each had money, none carried weapons; they were there to stay out of trouble and listen to the talk at the taverns, in the food stalls, at the games, and in the streets. They bought drinks, made new friends, and listened to the people grumble. Each day Asteraus met with each of them; he gathered the rumors and sniffed the air.

Rome was a complicated place; the old patrician families were constantly maneuvering among themselves for power but at the same time, the masses had to be kept happy. The rich lived for power and the poor lived for bread and the glory of Rome.

This system worked as long as each got what they wanted. Crassus provided the bread, and Caesar and Pompey the glory of conquest. They ruled Rome together but Crassus was in Syria now in his own quest for a kingdom, and Caesar and Pompey were like two hungry animals sizing up each other. They had been friends and allies, and Caesar had even given Pompey his daughter, Julia, for a wife, but she had recently died in childbirth. Caesar and Pompey were drifting apart now, and their ambitions were still alive. The ambitions of men never die.

* * * * *

The new Legions of Caesar were training in the cold of Ianuarius, all day, every day. Caesar's old veterans had responded in numbers and were turning the raw recruits into Roman soldiers; but time was needed and Caesar was impatient. He had no time. He was in the middle of a boiling cauldron with Pompey in the east, and the Gauls and Germans in the north. Rome was the mess it always was. Caesar's spies kept him informed; Asteraus came in twice to give Caesar his observations, then Caesar would send him back for more.

Spannus was doing another job for him too; Delmonus was in Pompey's camp and although Caesar had suspected it, now he was sure. Spannus and a hand-selected few had been observing his villa and the comings and goings there. Caesar wanted to know who was involved with him and Pompey. At least Gaul was quiet. By the spring, he would have his new Legions ready to march, whether it was to Gaul or Rome or to meet Pompey. No one knew what Caesar was thinking; no one ever did. Some of his generals saw bits and pieces, but Caesar trusted no man, with good reason.

* * * * *

"The tribes are coming in, Vercin, but we still have to deal with the Aedui. Young Aedui men are with us, but the leaders are a treacherous bunch. The old families still have much of the control over the feelings of the tribe. They control the Seine River and all the trade through their lands. Caesar has given them concessions that allow them to hold powers over the smaller tribes in there domain. We must go to the core of this problem;

we cannot fight a war against Rome with some of our own people not with us."

Vercingetorix was facing the bane of the Gauls: unity. If he couldn't have unity, he would at least have no treachery. The Aedui were good at treachery, they always had been. The coastal tribes and the closer ones in central Gaul were with the Arverni, The Belgae had been devastated a few years before, but Commius was always a threat to rise up. He had been granted dominion over parts of Belgae, and he had gone to Britannia with Caesar as some of his tribe had settled there. Other than Caesar, Commius didn't like Romans much. Ten Roman Legions were scattered across Gaul and as long as they were so, and as long as Caesar wasn't in Gaul, the might of Rome was paralyzed.

Vercin moved quickly. "Send Lucterius to the Ruteni and I'll go to the Bituriges. Cassive, you go the druidae. We'll surround the Aedui with support for our war and make them see the folly of continuing to support Rome." It wasn't easy but the Aedui reluctantly agreed to privately to help us and they sent hostages at our request; but you still could never be sure with that tribe.

News came that Crassus had been killed in Syria and that Rome was in turmoil. Crassus had protected Caesar in the Senate, but with him gone, Caesar's attention had to turn to Rome and the Senate. Our time was here. I rode to Vercin's farm. "Vercin, Crassus is dead and Rome is in turmoil. Caesar and his rivals will be tearing each other apart now, and he's on his way to Rome. Draius advises us that now is the time to strike. Caesar's Legions are scattered across Gaul and won't move until he orders them to; and he can't get to them without passing through us. The mountains are impassable and the local tribes there will have easy prey if he tries."

I think of Epacos that night on the mountain, my last night in my cave. He had saved my life so many times and now he lay at the foot of a cliff. I wonder if the Romans ever climbed down there. Could I climb down there? I had to get off this mountain if I were to live. I can't go down the paths; the cavalry has to be patrolling them. It's dawn now; the last of the eagle is in my stomach. I wash and pack my wounds again and put on my armor. I have my sword and my small shield; I'd need them where I'm going, but it was going to be hard going down that cliff with all that gear. I start to descend.

I walk cautiously using the boulders and hard places so I leave no tracks. I had come up that way and I know the way back. No Romans, no fresh tracks, just me in the thin air and hot sun; but I was moving. I reach that cliff at midday; I see Epacos's body down below and I think I can get down there, but carefully. That will be the worst part of this mountain then it'll flatten out. Where I go, I don't know, Romans will be all about. Are any of my people left? When Vercingetorix surrendered all the Aedui and Arverni were taken by Caesar and the other tribesmen were led away in chains. They're Roman slaves now. Who is left in Gaul? But first, I have to get to Epacos down below.

I make it down the cliff; it is hard and my wounds are bleeding again, but I make it. Epacos is where he had fallen; neither the Romans nor the birds have found him. The gear I had not taken with me that day, that day he died for me, would come in handy now. I might not need my helmet for a while but the tunic and canteen are welcome. There is a little stream nearby and trees and the place is out of the wind. I take limbs and such and make myself a nest under an outcropping from the cliff. This place is as safe as any I can expect to find, so I'll stay here for a while. I have water and wood for a fire and shelter from the autumn storms; and I have meat.

PAT MIZELL

CHAPTER IV

The Carnutes wanted the first blood. Their city Genabum was the center of Roman trade in the region. Caesar's quartermaster general was there and Roman merchants there represented a near stranglehold on Gallic goods. They bought our grain and iron for whatever they wanted to pay us. They then sold it to the Empire for whatever they wanted to charge. If the Carnutes attempted to sell their products elsewhere, they were met with the imperial might of Roman Legions. The Carnutes didn't have a land anymore; they were the slaves of Rome.

It began with a song. The ancient rallying song had led the Carnutes into many battles in the past. It started who knows where but it was picked up and carried all over Genabum. Soon the entire city was singing and the men started coming out of their homes and their taverns. They began the walk to the Roman warehouses and the army quarters. Slowly at first, and then they went into a run. The more that joined, the louder they sang and the faster they moved. When they got to the Romans, they started the killing. The warehouses were ripped open and every Roman in them died screaming. Then when the soldiers came, they died too. The Roman officer in charge, Caius Cita was turned into the Blood Eagle. The Carnutes had learned it from the northmen. The Roman wives, children, and everyone else of them who weren't killed were taken and sold to the Germani as slaves and disappeared into their forests forever. The uprising was now a revolt and the news shouted all over Gaul. From farm to farm and house to house, the shout went out that it was time to kill Romans, and it was done.

Caesar was on the march to Gaul when the courier met him. Pompey and he had settled for now and Caesar was on his way to quiet the rebellious tribes once and for all. His agreement with Pompey would not hold for long; he knew that. The two new legions were inexplicitly halted at midday and Caesar summoned his staff for a meeting. This was not Caesar's way; they were always announced in advance.

"Centurion, tell my generals what you told me and leave out no details."

"Yes, sir," said the courier. "The Gauls have declared war. They overtook the garrison at Genabum and killed all Romans; merchants, their families, and Caius Cita. They cut out his lungs and ribs and nailed them to a tree. They learned this from the Germani who learned it from the northmen; it is a declaration of war to the death. It's called The Blood Eagle."

Caesar marched through the Alpines into the subjected lands of the Helvetii before he was stopped. Mount Cevannes, through which he had to travel, was impassable. "Egius, you are supposed to be my best engineer. Get your men together and find a way over that mountain. Whatever it takes, you will have it. Find a way."

It was impossible; the passes had six feet of snow in them and it would be weeks before they cleared. However, the might of the Roman Empire was not just its fighting men; the men that built the bridges and roads and machines of war were the backbone of his army and they found a way, as they always did.

"It will take a lot of men, Caesar, but the concept is simple and it'll work. It will work but it will kill a lot of your men." Egius had a large platform of wood brought into the General's tent. On it was the mountain in clay and the passes in white sand. He explained his idea.

"At the head of the column we'll carry tents and provisions and will set up camps every mile. Food and warmth will be there waiting for your men. While they recover, my engineers will leapfrog another mile and set up another camp. In the meantime, another group of men will follow the first in the cleared path and then it's their turn to dig. Each man will know that he has to clear a mile of snow a day before he eats and rests for the night. As each group makes his mile, more men can come up and help. We'll clear our way over the mountain one mile at a time, with men working constantly. We have designed this to show you." With that, Egius had three wooden beams brought into the meeting. "We'll use a concept similar to a plow. These logs will be bolted together into a device that resembles a huge arrowhead. They'll have to be pulled by oxen and pushed by men but they will move the snow, and we can make all of these we need. Each plow will push snow aside, and then the next plow will have it easier and push the rest. We can clear a road for you over this mountain, but it will be brutal."

* * * * *

I found Vercin in the land of the Biturgenes. "My brother, Caesar is in our land. He has broken out of the mountains and he is in Arverni. Our people are terrified. He's burning their farms and houses. He's taking everything he finds and killing anyone in his way." We rode with the dawn, our warriors, and we, to our Arverni, This was what we wanted, and now it was the time for Romans to leave our lands or die. All of us were ready for this and the blood that would follow. Vercin sent Lucterius and his Sucones on a raid into the southern lands near Narbo, but Caesar countered and then we countered; we knew he would and he knew we would. We danced a bloody dance with each other. We would meet soon.

* * * * *

The Aedui were begging for Caesar's help. They were being raided from all around by the other tribes. No ally of Rome would be left in peace now; no haven for his legions would be left in our rear. They would be either with us or with our enemy; but the old men there still ruled, and they watched their people suffer. They begged Caesar to come. Caesar had a decision to make. If he ignored their calls, it would appear to all of Gaul that Rome couldn't protect them. If he went there, we could organize in Arverni. Caesar decided.

"Brutus, I'm leaving you in command here; don't make any stupid decisions. I'll be back soon but Caesar has to do what only Caesar can do. These tribesmen haven't seen the full force of Rome yet; they had their chance but that's over now. They think this is war? I'll show them Caesar's war and when they're all dead or on their way to Rome in chains, they'll know my might and Gaul will be a Roman farm. Keep my army alive until I'm back."

PAT MIZELL

He had started it all seven years ago when the Helvetii left their homeland and started their migration west; they had been north of the large mountains for generations but the German tribes were pushing hard on them and Rome wouldn't help. Rome wanted the Helvetii to die for them. When the tribesmen burned their farms and villages and started the move, the Romans attacked them, massacred them, and sent the remnants back to their barren lands. Caesar had all kinds of excuses but we knew what he wanted…he wanted our land and the lands of all the Gauls. So he started the killing.

And we did see, that summer, the will of Caesar. The man could do things others couldn't. Vercingetorix was a great man, and our warriors rode with all the fierceness that the Keltoi can, but it wasn't enough. When Caesar came at you it was with the full force of fifty thousand men with a single will; we saw the might of Rome.

In all my life, that was the first time I ever doubted Vercin. I had hunted the boar with him, though, and I knew his judgment was true. But for some reason, this plan seemed so unlike his strategy. Maybe he'd had enough. Maybe he wanted it over with. Maybe we underestimated Gaius Julius Caesar.

PAT MIZELL

CHAPTER V

The men on the barge saw them first. They were upriver from Genabum, bringing a load of grain for sale in the city's market. First, it was a cloud of dust in the west. Then as they drifted down the Loire, the cloud became bigger and closer. The more the men looked, the more it seemed to be moving toward them. Then they could see the riders out front, and slowly the lines of men appeared, and the banners. The banners of the Legions. Caesar was here.

Julius Caesar, Governor of all Gaul, sat on his horse on a hill above the town. His generals were with him and their faces were grim. This was the place where the Gauls had revolted and killed their soldiers and their merchants. This was the place where the Gauls had taken the lungs and ribs out of Caius Cita and nailed them to an elm tree in the city center for all to see. Now Rome was here with its answer.

"Aeneas, send the cavalry out. Have them ride a ring around this place and drive everything that moves back into the city. Kill anything that doesn't. When they're herded back in, I want those bridges blocked. No one is to escape. When I move, I want them all in there. And tell the men that the city will be theirs and everything in it; there will be no slaves made here today."

When the barge reached the pier, the city was in panic; the farmers had fled in front of the Romans and the city was packed. While people came in, others were fleeing and the bridges and gates were in turmoil. The men in the boat just kept going down the river. They saw the smoke that evening, after the screaming stopped.

* * * * *

Caesar gathered his forces from all over Gaul and he moved impossibly fast. When we thought he was here, he was there. Then we'd hear of him at another place, but we wouldn't find him. He left Decimus Brutus with the new Legions while he moved all over Gaul, bringing out his veterans from their garrisons. When he got them together, he attacked us, first at Genabum, where it had all started, and then the other cities of Gaul. He didn't just attack Genabum; he destroyed it. The townspeople didn't even try to defend themselves; they knew the revenge he would take. They fled over the Loire but Caesar was there, and he massacred them. Every man, woman, child, anything that moved was killed. The town was looted then burned and destroyed and Genabum paid the price of revolt. Caesar's wrath was not over; he slaughtered us at Vellaunodunum and Noviodunum and we couldn't stop him. Rome had turned its might and fury on Gaul and Caesar had put up his answer to the Blood Eagle.

* * * * *

"We can't beat them." Vercingetorix looked at us. "We've let ourselves go into battle under Caesar's rules and he's manipulated us like we were children. We started this war our way but he's put us in his trap and pulled his strings and our warriors are dying. Towns are dying. Farms are dying. Our people and our land are dying and despite the courage and desperation of our warriors, we can't win."

Vercin only said what we all knew; but we didn't know how to do it any differently. We would ambush Roman soldiers, sometimes with the numbers on our side, but they kept beating us. We couldn't fight them from our cities because they had the great engines of war. In the countryside, their discipline and training overcame the zeal and valor of the tribes. Only our cavalry was superior, but Caesar was bringing in Germani from across the Rhine now and horses for them from Hispania. Some of our people even rode for him. He seemed to anticipate our every movement and countered them. We lost every time. None of us knew what to do.

Vercin's great generals, Viridomarus and Eporedorix were there, as well as Sedullos, and the other chieftains of our tribes.

"We can't make our men what they're not," Vercingetorix stated, "but somehow we have to find a way."

That night, Vercin called us together. Others were there; men who had fought in the Roman lines. We talked. Some, like Brossix, had served in the Legions and Gerromir had been a slave in a garrison. We discussed the battles, and what had gone wrong, and why, and we looked at things as a warrior would; but Vercingetorix tried to make us think differently. "We have to look at ourselves the way Caesar looks at us. He knows our ways and he has spies to tell him of our movements but we can't do anything about that. We have to find his weaknesses and use them."

Draius too was there; he listened and asked questions Then, he told us what he thought. "We must look at the Roman Legion as it exists. There is a weakness, Vercingetorix, and you know what it is, but have let it slip away in your lust for blood. You've forgotten it's victory we're after, not the death of every Roman in our land. If they leave, we have won. If they die, Rome will just send more of them. We must make Rome want to leave Gaul. I'll tell you of Rome, its people, and this army, but you'll have to use your heads as well as your hearts and your swords if you don't want to perish.

"Rome is a complicated and treacherous place. It isn't the same city that it was when it was fighting for its own existence. They have defeated the Etruscans, Greeks and Carthage, and beaten back every one who's tried to destroy them. But, the Romans of then are gone and forgotten by the men who want ours now. The Roman army is a professional one now; not the one it was when it was a Roman farmer defending his land. We must make them go home; and the way to do this is by making it too expensive to be here; in money as well as blood. The Roman Senate cares not for these men's lives; they only want the gain of conquest. If they don't have that, they'll bring Caesar home.

"Rome is a snake pit, Vercin. The old families and the rich ones, like Crassus, live for power. Caesar has found the way to walk through the snares of the Senate. Crassus was the richest of them all and supported him, but he had enemies, as does Caesar. Pompey is loved by the people as Caesar is; those two great generals give Rome the glory and the riches of conquest. Between the three of them, they had control of Rome, but Crassus is dead now in Syria; the gold he wanted melted and poured down his throat. Pompey shares the power with Caesar; they are allies, for now. Caesar gave his daughter to him for his wife, but she is dead also. Friendship and power are rivals sometimes; the lust for one destroys the other and both of them are greedy men. Caeser walks a narrow path.

"If he can't serve Gaul up to the Roman people he'll be weakened, and Pompey will triumph. Caesar knows this; his future depends on what he does with you and our people. He'll kill everyone, including himself, before he faces this disgrace. Gaul will suffer; his men will suffer. Who will outlast the other? Our people say now that they are prepared for that, but will they sit by and watch their children cry in hunger? That is what Caesar is counting on…that we can't bear the pain he'll inflict on us, and we lose our restraint. If we do, we die. We Keltoi are not patient people and he knows this. I don't know what else to tell you. This is your burden."

* * * * *

Men started talking, and Brossix, at Vercin's urging, told us of the Legion's way. "I want to know everything you know, Brossix, and any of you other men who fought with or know of the Romans speak up. We aren't your royals anymore. We're in a war and we're your brothers, and talk to us so."

Gradually we came up with a plan. It wasn't anything new but we had gotten away from our strengths as Keltoi and Gauls. We couldn't just continue to snarl and scream and attack every time we saw Romans and depend on our manhood to win for us. It was the warrior instinct but our land was dying because of it.

Brossix spoke. "The soldiers are paid to serve Rome; that is their livelihood. They do what they're told because they trust their officers, and they gain from war. If they don't have wars and don't win, then there's no use for them anymore and they starve. The recruit gets a bonus when they enlist then they get drunk and spend it and they want more. And they get more; every month. Rome feeds them, clothes them, and only asks them to die for Rome. But then, their generals show them how to win and not die. That's why they trust them. They train constantly; first for four months before they're even given real weapons.

"They march every day and do what they're told or they don't eat that night. Then they are trained in weapons. Every

52

day the Roman soldier practices with wooden swords and shields. They are twice the weight of real ones so their arms grow strong. They march twenty miles every day, and practice and obey and they get used to it. Then they are introduced to the gladius, their short sword, and the Pilum, their lance, and they learn that their shields are weapons too.

"But the main thing is, they learn to unquestionably follow their orders. That is the strength of the Roman Legion. Each Legion has about five thousand men, and they all have swords; even the exempt ones; the carpenters, the engineers, the smiths and armorers. They all have swords and armor. A Legion has ten Cohorts of five hundred men each. The Cohort fights as a unit. Each Legion has a cavalry wing and siege weapons and wagons to carry their supplies, and six hundred mules. A Legion has everything needed to stay in the field and fight any battle anywhere. Whores go with them, and tavern keepers and spare horses and herds of cattle and grain to feed men and animals.

"When they go on a march they put enough food on their backs to last a few days and then they grab their weapons and they march day and night until their generals tell them to stop and rest, or fight. They follow their generals because they know that when it's all over they'll be turned loose to loot the conquered; this is their reward. When they defeat a people, they kill the men and sell the women and children to the slave merchants who travel with them. They all share in this; the generals and the men, then the men get drunk and the generals get richer and they go to the next.

"I made their weapons, Cassive, and they're not superior to ours. It's what they do with them that matters. The Roman gladius is not designed for cutting. It's made for killing. Cutting with a sword makes you bleed but a cut doesn't kill a man. It's the inside of him that has to be killed. A legionnaire is taught to stab you with his gladius; a few inches into a man will kill him. His cohorts will stand as a wall, each man protecting another with his shield. When our warriors attack that wall with their blood a boil, the Roman soldier will stick you. He'll go under the shield wall and over it with his gladius and use it like a short spear while we yell and scream and swing our swords and run around showing our valor. They just wait for you and kill you.

"Each man goes into battle with his sword and his shield; he will wear armor, each of them does, not just the rich and chiefs like us; we'll go wild and our swinging swords will slice them and batter them. They'll survive that. Their officers will watch and wait and the shield wall will stand. When they attack, the men each carry two pila. These lances can be thrown a long way and they'll go through a man. The Romans will throw them in a volley, and the officers watch. Then the horns are blown and the men look at the banners that tell them what to do next. They may form a wedge and charge or they may regroup and throw the other Pilum. If we charge at them, they go into their formation before we can get to them. If we counter with our own javelins, they go into their turtle formation with the men to the front and sides facing us with shields while the soldiers in the midst hold theirs above as a cover.

"And when they go into their shield wall each man lines up with his left foot forward, as he turns slightly to the side. His right leg is braced hard against the ground and they all hold their shields up, halfway covering the man on their right. Their shields are locked into one long wall. Each man has his gladius and will jab you under the shields, between the shields, or they'll reach over and stick you from the top. The main thing is the brute force the wall brings. The soldiers will push you or hold you and slam their shields into you and you'll get tired of that and do something stupid; then you die. Each line has other men behind it. When a legionnaire is hurt or becomes tired, another takes his place. The Roman army fights as one; one mind, one will, and one purpose; to wear you down for the kill. And all the time the officers are watching and assessing and when they see an opening the reserves are rushed in. It's not the number of men that's important; it's the discipline and the timing.

"All these things we know and all of their tactics can be countered and beaten. What makes them so effective is the speed they can move from one to the other. And the Roman generals don't mind losing men; they're cheap to them, compared to the gain of victory. The generals sit on their horses and watch. They understand the ebb and flow of battle and before you know it the horns blow and the banners show what the officers want next. A Roman general will never throw his men in at one rush; the reserve cohorts are sitting back there and then they'll be sent in at the crucial time at the crucial spot and Rome wins. That's what they're good at: waiting and winning."

We listened and we learned, but battle is a funny thing; when it starts, everything is forgotten in that first minute of killing and dying.

All the chiefs and kings came, and Vercin told them what must be done. "We've known how from the first; I don't know how we've let it get away from us. From the start, we knew the way but we let our balls and boiling blood rule our emotion. We have to starve them out of our land. They can't run around Gaul forever with their food on their backs; they must get it from our farms and warehouses, or they must leave. We'll burn the land and deny them and they'll go home. If we avoid battle, they get no glory or booty so they go home. This is our land and we'll make it very inhospitable to them. When they ride for our grain, we'll burn the land; when they offer battle, we'll ride away. When they look for a warm village to pass the night they'll find it destroyed. Our people must suffer to make the Romans suffer. We give our blood and lives and our people will have to give up their homes and farms and suffer with us. That is the way I see it."

They didn't like what Vercin told them to do, nor did we. We didn't like dying either. We couldn't beat the Romans; we had to make them leave. The fields, the barns, the villages, and everything Rome needed were destroyed. Our land burned. Everywhere we looked, there was smoke. The cattle and sheep in our fields were killed, the crops were burned, and the bridges were torn down. Whenever the Legions came to our towns, they found them empty. Gaul cried in pain. Our attacks began.

* * * * *

The Roman patrol trotted down the road; their horses were tired now. The day had been spent looking for food but all they had was a few chickens. To the right, beside a little copse of trees, was a cow munching on the grass.

"Centurion!" The outrider saw it first; there would be meat on their cook fire tonight. The twenty Romans rode for the cow as if it was a game. They threw their pila and yelled at it while Gerromir and his men came slowly out of the woods. The Romans never had a chance. We rode over them and the long swords of Gaul sung that day. That night there were twenty horses for Vercingetorix's cavalry and twenty Roman heads sitting on the ground, watching a cow roast over a Keltoi fire.

* * * * *

Gaul was burning. The fields were burning, the towns were burning, and our people were crying; and so were we. Every kernel of grain had been buried or destroyed in the fields. Dead sheep and cattle lay in their meadows. Homes that had been built by our fathers were pulled down. The thatch of the roofs, the timbers in the walls, the beds, the chairs, the chickens in the yards; all was denied to the Romans and to our people, too. They hid in the forests and lived like animals, scratching out an existence, while Gaul burned. It had to be like this. We could rebuild and replant but the Legions had to leave. We couldn't kill them all.

"The people hate us now, Vercin."

"I know, Cassive, but it's the only way. Everyone knew when we started how this would be; but making plans around a campfire with beer in your belly is different from a cold morning when you have to burn your neighbor's house. You knew it, I knew it, and all of you men knew it. And now, you don't want to do what has to be done? Think; what is our choice? Do we just let Caesar walk though our land and feed himself from our farms as if it was his right? Do we give him a nice house to sleep in at night? Should we just sit in our villages and wait for him to come for us?"

We were past the point of trying to explain to our people; they didn't care any longer about Romans, they just wanted to be left alone to live their lives. It made no difference to them who bought their grain or their iron because they didn't have it anymore to sell. We had called ourselves leaders when it was easy to be one, and now we had to endure the cries and hate of our own people. None of it made any sense, yet, it did. Every day, we went on the roads with our torches and axes; Vercin, me, all of us. We wouldn't ask the men to do what we wouldn't do ourselves. Every night we sat there in silence around our fires.

And our men still died. Caesar had brought in Germans to ride for him. They hated us anyway and now they were being paid to kill us. They learned to ambush us; it was easy, they just had to find a farm that hadn't been burned and wait. We'd be along and then we'd die. The hate spread. Soon everyone was hating; we hated ourselves.

* * * * *

"Can't we find some Romans to kill, Vercassive?" Gerromir didn't say much, but it was getting to him, this destruction of our own people. He had seen Rome destroy his Venetti lands by the sea and now he saw us destroying ourselves. So we went out; Gerromir and Vercin and me and some of our hard men. We knew how to lay an ambush too, and we did, causing the Romans to spread out looking for us. The more they had to ride the roads, the more they spread out, so we attacked their bases. Their supply bases were fat targets.

Vercingetorix and I lay behind the ridge line. The Romans knew better than to camp in the woods. They wanted the open spaces where they could watch for us, but they were men and men couldn't always stay vigilant. There were wagons, lots of wagons, lots of mules, and a herd of cattle. We knew those wagons would be full of grain and weapons, and the tents of the generals and their drink and their captured booty. We had been laying this trap for days now. Our riders hid in the woods and watched the movements of the Roman patrols. We could tell by how much they carried how long they'd be gone; so we waited and watched, and learned their habits. For if anything, the Roman army was consistent. We spread them out; we were everywhere and now they were too, looking for us. Some of us were waiting behind. The patrols would leave at dawn and then the camp would settle into its routine. The exempt men would be there, repairing the weapons, making engines of war, taking care of the animals and all of the usual occurrences things that went on everyday in a Legion. These men could fight; there was no question of that. They were all tough men whether they were the men of the front lines or just the men who kept the army going. But there was a difference; they weren't ready to when we hit them.

We came over the ridge top and out of the forest. We weren't carrying shields or screaming like we usually did; we were far past that. We weren't looking for a battle; we were looking for a killing. We ran with our spears and swords in our hands and our hate in our hearts. We wanted to kill and destroy and take out our self loathing on others for a change. It felt good. We killed over a hundred of them that day; sooner or later that day. We pissed on their food, and that felt good, too. When we left we burned their wagons and ran off their mules, and we took the cattle back to our people. That day we were Keltoi warriors again. But Rome was still here the next day.

* * * * *

"You must leave, my love. Things will get worse."

Ladia just stared at Vercin. "Where would I go?" We were raiding close by and had gone to the farm. I left them alone and took the boys for a ride; but I knew what they would be saying. Vercin had told me of his plans during our ride there. Commius had sent word to us; some of his people had gone to the green isles and Ladia would be safe with them. However, Ladia was a farm girl and knew only Gaul. She didn't want to leave.

"It's not going stop anytime soon, Ladia. I wish all of our people could leave but they won't. There's no point for you to stay here. There's no farm for you to tend; most of the livestock is dead or running wild in the forests, and you know what the Romans would do with my family. You'll be safer with Commius and I can war without the worry for you and the children. There won't be much to eat here either, for a long time, I think. It'll probably be winter before the Romans leave. They'll stay as long as they can scrounge food from our land, but by winter, there won't be anything left. We're attacking their resupply from Massilia and Cisalpinia and our rivers are full of destroyed Roman boats; but they'll stay until the last. Next winter will be very hard, even with them gone. There'll be no crop this year and next before we can replant and harvest. You'll be back then; I promise to come for you when we can live again."

She didn't look too happy when I came back. Not like she did when she first saw Vercin that day. All of our leaders were having the same conversations with their families. We had to be free to fight and die. She finally agreed; she just didn't do it.

* * * * *

Vercingetorix's mood was black in those days. People were dying because of him and this hung heavy. The only times he felt better were when we were doing some killing; and we did a lot of that. That day, after we left the farm, we rode to Brossix's home. His was a small village, I forget the name now, but he was the blacksmith there before this all had started, and it was a home to us. His wife Mirandia was like a mother to us. Neither of us remembered our own mother, they had both died when we were small.

Brossix was there in his shed, honing an axe that he favored. Not many men could fight with one, but he could and he liked it. Today was a lull in our days of deaths and it was almost like the old times when we rode and hunted and enjoyed living; but there would be a tomorrow, we knew. Gerromir was there too; he had no home to go to. After Caesar's navy had destroyed his land, there was nothing left for him in Venetti. His people had lived on the sea. They made their living fishing and trading Gaul's goods with other lands, but no more. Only Rome could have the essence of our land now.

Mirandia had a mutton stew for us that night, and there was a barrel of ale. We sat by the fire later, no one saying much, deep in their own thoughts. Then the next morning we rode. Gerromir knew where there were Romans to kill. There was just the four of us, but together we were formidable. There were only a dozen or so Romans and they were supply troops. We were lucky; they were escorting two mules carrying casks of wine. That night we had roasted some turnips and drank some general's wine and two Roman mules became free Gauls.

PART II

AVARICUM

PAT MIZELL

I must get stronger; the Horned One has told me what I must do. But first, I have to survive. It's cold on this mountain, but not as cold as my people are in their graves; or Vercin in his cage. There will be others like me; Commius escaped Alesia, and Lucterious will be somewhere. But Ladia is alone now, wherever she is. I'll find her and the others, the ones still alive and not Roman slaves. My will has returned, Epacos has seen to that. I sharpen my sword and burnish my armor; I eat and mend and hide here, in this hidden crevice. Every Roman I kill will be Caesar. Every step I take will be toward him. I hope there are plenty of both.

PAT MIZELL

CHAPTER VI

Avaricum was the most beautiful of our cities. It was in the land of the Bituriges and its storehouses were full of the grain that Caesar's army so desperately needed. We had been forced to harvest early but it had been a bountiful one and Caesar knew that if he took Avaricum that he would eat and we wouldn't. We had burned and destroyed over twenty of our towns and hundreds of farms and the Romans were suffering. It was working. Avaricum stood in front of them now.

Their people begged us to spare it. It was on a hill and surrounded by rivers and marsh. The forty thousand men and women who lived there said their city was impregnable and they'd fight. Vercin wasn't sure but they finally convinced him, or seemed to. Some of the chiefs of other tribes argued for it too and Vercin gave in. We should have burned it.

Vercin told me later, "If we're going to take this gamble, then I want more out of it than just Caesar walking away hungry. We'll let him throw his army against its walls while ours ignores him. If the Avaricums hold, then we'll crush him against those walls. And if they don't, we'll walk away from them. The Romans have to be getting hungry now and when a man gets hungry he starts to doubt and when that happens an army will come apart. They've only known victory till now; we'll see how they handle the other." We had Caesar at last, if Avaricum held. We'd destroy him and send him home. The key was the will of the people of Avaricum.

We met with their elders and Vercin informed them, "You'll be on your own here; I won't put my army behind your walls. Can you fight off Caesar with your townsmen? Because I won't gamble all of Gaul for your city." We knew what they would say, and they did, and we thought they could hold if their will was there. If they did hold, then we'd have Caesar's Legions between the anvil and the hammer. "I'll give you some men but you'll live or die by your own resources, and Rome is formidable. You must be prepared for that army and all the might of Caesar's Legions. Can you do this? If you can't, you'll die." They said they could. Men are always bravest before they've seen death up close.

Vercingetorix and I sat on our horses and watched the wagons going through the gate. The harvest of the Bituriges was bursting the walls of the city already and more was coming in. The farmers were coming in too. A Keltoi farmer was more than just a farmer. He was a warrior defending his home. Vercin put ten thousand of our men behind those walls and the forty thousand people who lived there would fight too if they wanted to live.

The Bituriges were a subject tribe to the Aedui. Their lands were large and fertile and they were important to our cause. Vercingetorix had gone to see them when we first went to war, and under pressure, they had declared for us. Their faith was shaky before, but they had declared for us and we had to help them here. We had heard rumors of them withdrawing from our coalition and becoming friends of Rome again. They didn't know it then, but many of the Aedui were helping us now and we hoped to have their warriors soon. There were some political obstacles to overcome first. We just had to hold the tribes together until then.

Avaricum was located between two rivers and there were marshland and swamps all around the city. There was only one way in and it was a narrow way. The walls of Avaricum were tall and strong. Caesar had no other option but to storm the city over that narrow plain unless he built bridges, and we weren't going to let him do that. We were beginning to feel good about this. Vercin wanted to show all of Gaul that we would protect the smaller tribes from Caesar.

"Avaricum is the cheese, Vercassive, and Caesar is my rat. When he goes for it, we'll spring the trap and hit him with our army. There is nowhere he can go and we'll crush him here against those walls if these people will hold. This time the battle will be on my terms." He was getting more and more confident every day; it seemed like a good strategy. I kept thinking of what

Draius had said about making the Romans go home instead of trying to kill them all.

* * * * *

Caesar's army advanced toward Avaricum. He had conquered Genabum, Vellaunodunum, and Noviodunum. He had forced us to pursue him, but his supplies were low now and his men needed a rest. This would be a good place for both when he had destroyed the forty thousand Bituriges that lived there.

The Roman generals met, as usual, at dawn that morning. It was different from Caesar's usual meeting; he was quiet and pensive and wanted to hear what others thought. This would not be the typical Roman battle, where the Cohorts formed and the generals orchestrated their movements to victory. Avaricum would take some thought.

Have no doubt: Caesar was a magnificent general, and he never doubted himself. Part of his genius was recognizing that every new challenge required a unique solution. Avaricum sat like a rock. There were rivers and marshland around it. The approach to it was through a narrow neck of land that had no cover for the Legions; but it must be done. Gaul must see that no part of itself was safe from the Roman will.

The discussions went on all day, and the next. Thoughts and ideas were thrown around, while Caesar listened. He just sat in his chair and listened. Several things were obvious. Cavalry was of no use. The land was marshy and wet and a horse could move no faster than a man could. Yet they still ate and had to have forage. If Caesar sent them away, he would be naked to raids from Vercingetorix's riders.

Finally he spoke. "This is a battle for my engineers. Battle tactics are of no use when attacking a wall. Men must reach it, climb it, and then kill everything they meet. I have no doubt that my men can do this, but I don't want them slaughtered. We have to get them in there."

The Roman army was not just an army of swords. There were geniuses in it. They had built the roads of the empire through mountains and hostile environments. They had built the bridges over the rivers of Gaul and had gotten Caesar's armies through the snow covered Alps. This was just another problem to be solved. However, Caesar had to feed them in the meanwhile.

The engineers met with Caesar. They had a plan to present to him and as usual, Egius had made a model of the terrain. His men brought it in and sat it on Caesar's table. It was fashioned on several planks that were nailed together and on it there was blue clay representing the two rivers, green clay showing where the marshes were, and the hills around were shown by brown and built to show their heights. In the middle was Avaricum and before it was the neck of land that approached it, where the Legions had to advance.

Caesar watched and listened while Egius showed him how his machines would conquer the problem. It was Roman elegance at its best in its simplicity. Engineers don't have moments of brilliance. They just take a problem and break it down into conquerable bits and pieces, then show how their tools will work to do this. This was no different.

"It's not practical, Caesar, to build bridges over those rivers and attack the city there. The walls are surely not as formidable there, but that's for a reason. To build a bridge underneath the range of their arrows and other missiles would be a nightmare to your men and you'd lose a lot of them. Neither can we go through the wetlands with speed enough to survive the same. And to attack the main wall, which is the only real alternative, will be carnage. Your Legions have to tear that wall down or go over it and it is eighty feet above the lowest part in front."

Caesar watched the engineers pour the sand little by little on the model, until the mound approached the wall. Once it passed a certain point the distance from the ground to the top of the wall was significantly less. Egius showed him how the vineus would advance before the ramp with men behind it to fight off raids. He showed him the wooden tunnels that would move men forward and he showed him the towers that would advance at the end. Caesar could see it. The concept was simple, but elegant in its simplicity. They would build a ramp that took them to the top of the walls of Avaricum. Then, when the ramp got there, they would move the towers along it until they could throw down their gates onto the top of the wall and allow the Legions to pour across into the city.

It was a creeping approach where a mound of dirt was built behind a moving wall called a vineus that kept the men partially hidden and safe. The wall advanced as the mound advanced. It was just hard and brutal work. Men would shovel dirt into buckets and take them forward, pour it on the ground and then do it again. Forty thousand men and forty thousand buckets carrying dirt, piling it until the mound was close enough to the city's walls, and as high as them, for men to go over the walls with their swords.

There was only one problem. "How long will this take?" Caesar asked. He got his answer the way an engineer would give the answer. One bucket held this much dirt. Forty thousand buckets would have to be filled by forty thousand men with forty thousand shovels. The distance from the Roman lines to the Gallic wall was measurable. It was a matter of mathematics.

"You're telling me that if my men work for sixteen hours a man, all my men, that we can be at the wall of Avaricum in a month?"

"Yes," responded Egius. So the siege began.

Julius Caesar, Governor of all Gaul, commander of fifty thousand Roman soldiers, Consul of Rome, and hero of the people and his men, sat in his tent. He was alone; he had a glass of wine. The remnants of his dinner sat on the table next to the model of Avaricum.

So all I have to do is feed forty thousand men for thirty days and fight off the raids from the city and the army of Vercingetorix, wherever it is, while this mound of dirt moves forward. I guess it could be worse. If I had to keep the ocean parted for thirty days, it would be worse. If I had to march through the heavens for thirty days, it'd be worse. If I had to fight off thirty armies for thirty days, it'd be worse, he thought to himself.

Part of Caesar's genius was his confidence in himself and the iron will he had once he had made a decision. Another part of his genius was convincing others that he was right. This convincing was not done by his words but by his demeanor. Still another part of his genius was in picking his generals and trusting them to do what he required of them. They met that next morning and he told them what had to be done.

"Here is the plan; laid out on this table. If there are any doubts I want to hear them now but I think it's sound. I trust my engineers' judgment as I trust each of you to do your part. The Aedui will feed us; it won't be a feast for the next month but we can get by. The countryside is wrecked but there are hay and grain somewhere, and there are pigs in the forests. You just have to find the food. Vercingetorix is out there somewhere but he won't fight us.

"Aeneas, your cavalry is useless to me sitting here, but you can patrol the roads and chase the Gauls away. Those worthless bastards will be hiding and shivering somewhere and complaining of the weather; Gaul is a mess right now so they won't need much excuse to lay up. They'll ride away from you when they see you but kill a few for entertainment when you can. The men need it; they're going to be hungry for a while and without their wine and something to hump they're going to be in foul moods anyway."

"Sir," the young general asked, "how can we move so much dirt in a month's time?"

"One shovel full and one bucket full at a time," Caesar answered. "It's a matter of mathematics. We put down a layer of dirt and then cross it with a layer of trees, and you keep repeating that until you get far enough and high enough. You just get me the wood and the dirt. Long hours are the best thing to cure short rations. Just make sure your men know who's causing this misery for them. They're right behind that wall over there. Give my men someone to hate so they won't hate you and me.

"Now we start. Cut down those trees over there," he pointed, "and make them into implements and towers and engines of war. Make me a wall to shield my men while they move forward. I'll get you the food; just keep those fucking Gauls off my back."

Epacos is starting to stink. I've cut off most of the meat and dried it in the sun, but the birds and I fight for it. I'm stronger now, and my wounds are scabbed over and pink and the sun is making me hard again and tomorrow I'll wash and shave. I may die on this mountain, but if I do, I'll die looking like an Arverni warrior, not some scraggly piece of garbage. I'm getting restless and while I sit here, Vercingetorix is in a Roman cage; it's killing me. I wonder where the others are. I think Commius escaped; I saw him riding as if the gods were after him when we broke on the shield wall of Caesar. I don't know about the others, most of our brothers were with Vercin inside the walls of Alesia.

I killed a Roman yesterday. I was moving around on my mountain when I saw the shepherd's hut. He was behind it and skinning a hare and I wouldn't have seen him but for his woman coming out the door. I went down last night when they were sleeping. She was a Gaul; I don't know what tribe because she died screaming right after I cut the man's throat and sliced off his balls. They had food though and now I've got grain and a few other things. He must have been a deserter because I found armor and a sword inside the hut. Lot of good it did him in there. His helmet makes a good stew pot.

PAT MIZELL

CHAPTER VII

Our scouts had come in. "The Romans have moved into position. They're there, all ten Legions. Their banners stand just a mile from Avaricum's front door." Vercin seemed content that day. The scouts showed us how the Romans were deployed, though there wasn't much doubt where they'd be. He talked, but we knew what to do. It just felt good hearing it from him. "Avaricum sits on a hill with a river behind it and a river beside it, and marshland all around it. On a hill, just a mile from Avaricum's highest wall sits the Legions of Rome. There is a valley between them and the town and they'll have to go down it then up the other side, and then they have to climb up that wall. And while they're doing that we'll be hitting at them. At night, hit their camps; when they get close to our walls cover them with arrows, rocks, and hot water if they get close enough.

"When Caesar's patrols go out hit them. When they're cutting hay for their horses, hit them. Hit them then get out of there. We'll bleed them a while. When they are hung up on the wall of Avaricum, we'll crush them against it. They've killed our people and now we're going to kill them. And if Rome sends more men we'll kill them too."

I could almost feel what the others were thinking. It sounded more like Gerromir talking than it did Vercin. We were all full of ourselves then. We had the Romans pinned down at last. There would be no more miraculous marches for Caesar now. We had fifty thousand people behind the walls of Avaricum and a lot of them could fight. And we'd move our army behind Caesar and he couldn't escape, unless he killed all of us first.

Vercin didn't talk this way to the other chiefs. He acted reluctant to spare Avaricum when he spoke to them. I think he was just trying to scare them. We could win this fight. Caesar could try all he wanted to but he couldn't storm that wall and when his men were spent we'd hit them from their rear. For now, we'd just sit out here a day's march away and wait. We had the position and the food, this time. The only thing I didn't understand was how Caesar let himself get lulled into this trap. But great men seem to get arrogant at times.

A Roman Legion went to war with everything it needed to wage a siege. The great missile-throwing machines were broken down and carried on wagons, ready to be reassembled. New ones could easily be made from trees. Wagons of saws, axes, shovels, sleds, buckets, and hammers and nails moved with a Legion. There were ten Legions at Avaricum. The Roman camp was on a hill and a mile away was another hill with Avaricum on it behind a tall and thick wall.

Caesar began to build his ramp. It was a simple but methodical process. Men dug into the hills around and other men shoveled the dirt into sleds and buckets and carried it to the front lines. Others cut down trees. They poured the dirt out, men smoothed it down, threw in the trees, and more men brought more dirt. More trees were cut down and hewn into lengths that would be fashioned into towers. A tall and portable wall called a vinae was made of tree limbs and light timbers and leather and roped together into a moving screen that was pushed out further each day to make room for more dirt and more men. Roman cavalry patrolled the flanks and fended off the Gallic raids that came out of the gates of Avaricum. Sentries were doubled at night and stood watch over the Roman camp. The people of Avaricum stood behind their wall and watched. Caesar was coming for them.

* * * * *

Aeneas planned his raid. He had four thousand horsemen that he could send out. Not all were well mounted, and some were tribesmen or Germans, but they could do what he wanted. He needed grain, barley, and peas for the men and hay for the horses He also needed any pigs or cattle that he could find. Fifty thousand men, six thousand mules, and five thousand horses eat a lot every day. There were thirty of those days ahead of them until Caesar broke this city.

The countryside around the Roman army was unknown to Caesar's scouts. There were farms out there, and storehouses of grain and other foodstuffs; they just had to find them. In order to find them, they had to ride the roads through the marshes and forests. Unfortunately for them, that was where the Gauls were. Aeneas had to find the food and protect the men he sent to get it. He knew there were thousands of braided warriors out there waiting for him. But it had to be done. Aeneas gave his orders.

"Marcus, take your Cohort and fifty wagons. Ten soldiers for each wagon should keep the flies away. Put a couple of stout woman slaves on each for the field work but for the love of the gods don't let them around the scythes at night or they'll be cutting off Roman balls instead of Gallic wheat. Take the Remi scouts too. And remember, this isn't a killing party. Bring back food and leave the killing for another day. These Bituriges have their harvest hidden somewhere; cut a few throats if you have to, but find it. And don't fuck around, Caesar will be all over me if we don't start putting something in his pot. The Aedui and Boii are dragging their asses about getting supplies to us and Egius's diggers are eating like horses."

Aeneas sent another group of riders out that day. A German tribesman that the Romans called Urdus had brought a hundred or so of his raiders to Caesar. Aeneas didn't send any wagons or slaves with them; they were to find the storehouses and bring information back. They couldn't ride with Romans or Remi as they all hated each other; but the Germani were useful, for what they did, which was mainly killing.

Caesar's Legions kept digging and building the ramp to Avaricum. The engineers made use of the wagons and mules of the army; mules couldn't dig but they could carry. The problem was feeding them; the men and the mules. They were working fourteen to sixteen hours a day and they ate a lot. Caesar had started a rotation system where men could do sentry and other duties every few days to give them a rest, but still it was grinding them.

Caesar walked among them and spoke with them. Each morning, after his staff meeting, he would go to the ramp. He ate with the men; the same thing they ate. The foraging parties had meager results; sometimes they didn't return. Men would die for Caesar but now they were hungry and wearing out. They continued to dig, the mules carried the dirt, and the ramp grew every day.

Yet, all of that wouldn't be enough. Caesar needed the food and support of his allies; the Aedui and the Boii. Their lands had shared in the bountiful harvest of the past year too, and could feed his Legions. It was just a matter of getting it from their storehouses to his camp at Avaricum. He had the wagons and the oxen and Roman roads to move it on.

Bibracte was the great city of the great tribe of the Aedui, and for the last fifty five years, the Aedui had enjoyed special status in the transalpine area of Gaul. They were *Friends of Rome and the Roman Senate*. This official status made them the favored ones of Rome. This gave them the right to control trade between their subject tribes and Rome and the control of the rivers that ran through them. It also gave them the right to tax.

The Aedui had long contended with the Arverni for supremacy in central Gaul, but Rome had weakened the Arverni and made the Aedui the surrogate of Rome. Rome gave them these rights and protected them from the other tribes and all it asked it return was anything it asked for. The Aedui gave everything they were asked to give. Now they were asked to feed Caesar's Legions.

The Germani returned. Aeneas stood and watched Urdus and his men ride in; there appeared to be no casualties, but there was a line of slaves walking behind the mercenaries. Aeneas went to his tent and the Germani leader soon came to give his report.

"What news, Urdus? And where did you pick up those Gauls? It doesn't look like you had to fight for them."

"We didn't, General, they were walking down the road about a day's ride from here. We herded them up and saw that they had been slaves already. They took us to where they had been that day. There were burned wagons there and dead Romans; a lot of them. They had been stripped of their armor and weapons and appeared to have died fighting around and behind the wagons; which were empty except for some scythes."

It was Centurion Marcus's patrol; it was the only one out. "Did you cremate the bodies?"

"We did," said the black bearded warrior. "We left everything else."

Aeneas dismissed the Germani, who hesitated at the entrance of the tent and asked, very tentatively, "And the slaves, sir? Who gets them now?"

The Roman general said, without looking up from his writing, "They've seen Rome defeated. Kill them."

* * * * *

The Roman soldiers were sitting around the cookfire; they were tired, and the boiled peas and grain of their meal was now just a memory. There was little wine and it was bad. The men knew that in eight hours they would be digging again.

One of them, the young one, was grumbling to himself, "I didn't enlist in the Legion to dig a fucking hole in the ground. We're sitting here in this shithole with no drink, no women, and not enough food. We dig holes in the ground and then carry the dirt and pile it in a mound. How long is this going to go on?"

A man looked up and stared at the young soldier. "Until that pile of dirt reaches that wall. Behind it is the food and drink you talk about. When we reach it we'll kill the people in it then we'll lie on our asses and get drunk and they'll lie in this fucking hole we're digging."

* * * * *

"Who are you sending into Avaricum?" I was curious about who Vercin would pick for his leader there.

"It's got to be one of their own, Cassive, one of the Bituriges. Do you have any thoughts?" Vercingetorix was putting ten thousand of our men behind those walls. Most of the young men of the Bituriges were with us already, and the forty thousand people that lived there weren't warriors. They could carry water and cook food and mill about wailing and crying but that was all.

"Montanius is a good fighter, but more importantly he's a good miner. And with that mound of dirt coming, someone who understands digging might be good. Quarimus is experienced too. Most of us just know how to swing our swords and yell; probably him or another steady man who can keep those people quiet. They're going to get really panicked when Caesar gets close but I'm not sure I want just one man in charge, Cassive. It might be better to have our fighters under our orders that a local man can't change. But a man experienced with mining is a good idea. Let's ask around and see who we have. Maybe we just put groups of men in with strict missions and let it rest at that. Maybe a calm man like Bituminous, respected, who can manage things while our men stand and fight."

* * * * *

"Where is my food?" Caesar stared at his generals. "These men are killing themselves for me and I can't feed them. I go among them every day. I eat the same ration they get. It's swill and not much of that."

One by one, the officers spoke up. "The fields are empty, sir. The storehouses are empty. There is no one out there except Vercingetorix's warriors, who we don't see until they start killing us. My men go out and their mules come back alone." Tarius was a veteran general. He wasn't afraid to tell the truth to Caesar, and Caesar knew it was the truth.

"And the Aedui and the Boii? Where is the food they promised?" No one spoke. "What is going on with them? Aeneas, what do your Remi scouts say?"

"Caesar, two days ago, a convoy of wagons from Bibracte was ambushed. Two hundred wagons of grain were lost. The Aedui were camped for the night and Vercingetorix rode in and took everything."

"Is that what the Remi tell you or what you know?"

"I rode there, Caesar, and it was as they said. All the food was gone."

"How many Aedui died defending it, Aeneas?"

* * * * *

Ladia and Mirandia came to our camp. Ladia had been staying with Mirandia since the farm was torched. Vercin was happy to see her of course but that didn't stop him from going on a tirade about Ladia traveling on the roads.

"Ladia, you have to understand, it's not just your life. It's the lives of the children you endanger. If you are captured or killed, they'll have no one. I want you in the islands with Commius.

You too, Mirandia." Mirandia left to find Brossix; she had made him a pair of doeskin boots. Vercin went on.

"Do you think I can fight when I know you're in danger? If Caesar captures you, my love, he'll torture you in front of all of Gaul. Do you think I can sit here and ignore that? The man tries every day to make me do something stupid and it's hard enough for me to ignore him. It's hard for my men to understand why we don't attack their camp. I have to hold this army together until the time is right." He took her into his arms and his tent. Then she left and I didn't see her again until we were in Alesia.

* * * * *

"I speak for Caesar and he's not happy." The elders of the Aedui were afraid, and showed it. Decimus Brutus, the Prefect of the Ninth Legion, and patrician of Rome had ridden into their city with two Cohorts of the toughest men of Rome. "I have the might of Rome waiting for me to call them here, Divaticus. You promised Caesar grain and cattle and now you sit here shaking and cowering while our men are without. You should be shaking. These thousand men with me are hungry, and they're angry, and they'd like nothing better than to tear apart your town. Please me, Divaticus. Tell me something that I want to hear."

"We sent you food, Brutus, but they attacked us and stole it. Food is not that easy to replace in such quantities, but we're trying."

"Bring me the men who led this convoy, the leaders. I want to talk to them myself. I want to hear about the great battle they put up. I want to visit the homes of the men killed in that raid, and console their widows. Take me to them, Diviciacus. Then we'll go to your home and see how much your family is suffering and starving; like our men are, I'm sure. How many have died helping us, Divaticus? Are your promises to Caesar being kept? He'll ask me that, you know. He'll ask me what I think. It's very important that you convince me."

* * * * *

Caesar sat alone in his tent. *I don't like what I'm seeing and not seeing. The Boii are one thing; they have had a rough winter. But the Aedui? I can smell something with them. Brutus will sort it out; if not, then Aeneas certainly can. He'll squeeze those bastards until they*

79

squeal and enjoy doing it. I'll tell him to take the Germani with him; they'd like that.

Our scouts were watching the Roman camp, and giving us reports. They said that Caesar rode among the men every day; his white horse and red cloak couldn't be missed. He even took meals with them at noon. He seems imperturbable, they'd say, but his men must be exhausted and hungry. We knew what was going in there and it wasn't much. Our men in the Aedui were finding ways to circumvent the orders of the old men. The wagons of grain were few, and their foraging parties weren't finding much. We knew that.

We were hitting their patrols when they went out; and bleeding them. Caesar's army was pinned between ours and the walls of Avaricum. What I wondered was, would Vercingetorix let them leave, if they decided to? Vercin wasn't saying much those days, even to me. I thought he was unsure but didn't want anyone to see it. The tribes of Gaul had to have confidence in him or they would just go home. Or, worse than that, just strike out with their chiefs to attack Romans somewhere else. It was hard for our people to stay together and to sit and take orders. They would much rather be riding and killing.

* * * * *

Aeneas reported, "They're dragging their feet, Caesar. I went to their homes and storehouses; they have grain, there are cattle in their fields but the Aedui have all kinds of excuses. I don't know if it's fear of retribution from the other tribes or dissention amongst themselves; their leaders wouldn't admit either; they just have banal excuses."

Caesar looked at Brutus, and around the tent at his other generals. "Well, we're soon to find out. Aeneas, take enough cavalry to defend yourself, not to start war but to show I'm serious. I want you to go to every noble family; ask them how many hectares of land they own. Quintus Barius, you're my quartermaster. You tell Aeneas how much to demand. From each farm, I want wagons of grain. I want cattle, I want swine. I want these things this week.

"Aeneas, you tell their nobles and elders that this is not a matter for discussion or negotiation or excuse. At the end of this week, you send me a rider with a dispatch. Tell me in that dispatch how many wagons are on the road to Avaricum. In that same dispatch, you tell me how many men you need to destroy Aedui if the wagons don't come. And tell the Aedui this: when I send these men to you I'm sending the Germani also. Tell the Aedui that their instructions will be to kill every old man they can find. Anyone with grey hair or a bald head is going to die. We'll see who has the influence in that tribe. If it's not the men I've been dealing with, then I want to know who they are. And if the people I vested with my support have lied to me, they'll die; tell them that.

"Tell them that if the Aedui are not the friends of Rome they claim to be, that they are of no use to Rome. They'll lose their privileges and they'll pay taxes like the rest of Gaul does. But first, some of them will die. Tell them that I'm going to make some new friends. Tell them that I'll open their back door to Germani. Tell them that after Urdus takes his bald and grey trophies that he'll go back to his lands and show them to the other Germani and tell them how rich that land is. And he'll tell them that Caesar will not object to anything they want in the land of the Aedui."

PAT MIZELL

I left my nest there on the mountain yesterday and spent last night in a secluded spot I found on the next one. I'm looking for Gerromir; if he survived, he'll come back to these mountains. It's where he was before he joined us a year ago. Him and some other renegades. If anyone lived after Alesia, it would be he. If he's in these mountains I won't find him, he's like a ghost, but he'll find me.

I am Vercassivellaunus of the Arverni again, not the miserable wreck that hid on that mountain. Before I left it, I washed and braided my hair. I shaved with my knife and polished my armor with sand. My sword is sharp again, and I have new horsehide boots and my wounds are healed now. I'm lean and tanned and have my armbands and torque and I'm ready to go to war again. There will be others like me still around.

PAT MIZELL

CHAPTER VIII

We could see everything from the hill. It was a long way away, but we could see it all. We sat on our horses in some trees high above Avaricum. The Roman camp was to our left and the earthen ramp leading from it was getting closer to the walls of the city. Gerromir was with us, as well as Quarimus, a man who had built and managed iron mines all over Gaul.

"How long, Quarimus?"

The rugged old man looked at Vercingetorix. "Another two weeks. They've come almost half way in and when they finish filling up that low area there'll be less dirt to have to haul. They'll bring it to the wall and when they're ready for the assault they'll roll those towers and wooden turtles right up there."

Brossix was with us, too. "The Romans are at their best in open ground, where they use their training and tactics, but they know how to assault a town too. With all of that building going on down there, they have wooden walkways for the soldiers to move to the front. They'll run those down there to the end of the ramp and fill them with men all the way back up to their camp. Then they'll roll those two towers along the ramp until they're in position. When the men from the turtles start running up the stairs, the engineers at the top will drop the front door of the towers down onto the top of the wall, and fifty thousand Romans will go into Avaricum."

"Vercin," said Quarimus, "I can dig tunnels from inside Avaricum that go under the wall just as fast as the Romans can dig and move the dirt for the ramp. When a miner digs a tunnel he's usually going through rock, but still we build wooden props to keep them from caving in. That ramp's nothing but loose dirt and trees. If we build tunnels under it, prop them up with beams, and fill them with dry wood then we've set our trap. When Caesar's ramp gets as far as we want it to go, we light a fire, and the whole thing goes up. The timbers and the beams catch fire and all the burning sucks the air out of the tunnel and then the ramp sinks in on itself."

"Will this work?" Vercingetorix stared hard at Quarimus.

"If it's done right."

We looked around at each other, probably all wondering the same thing.

"Cass?"

"I don't know of these things, Vercin."

"Gerromir, Brossix?" None of us spoke because none of us knew. When we rode back to camp, Quarimus got some of his miners and they gave us a little exhibit. It didn't take them long to dig a small tunnel into the side of a hill. They put staves upright in it and filled it with limbs and firewood. They had Brossix, the heaviest of us to stand above the spot where the tunnel ended and stomp the ground. It held. Quarimus told us to go and come back in an hour; and he set the wood in the tunnel on fire.

Vercin and I went to his tent. He always had a keg of beer, and we talked about a lot of things: Ladia, Caesar, our men and their moods, and Avaricum. Then we went back to Quarimus's tunnel. Smoke was pouring of a hole about ten feet away from the mound. Quarimus asked Gerromir to walk to where Brossix had stood; he was a much smaller man than Brossix. When he did, the ground started sinking and collapsing around him while we stood there in shock.

We were back in Vercin's tent, all of us leaders now. "Take anybody you need, Quarimus, the city should have the shovels and barrows and the wood."

"It's also got forty thousand whining and crying citizens who can be useful and haul the wood in and the dirt out," said Gerromir. He was never easy on anyone, including himself.

"I'm glad you thought of that," said Vercingetorix. "Because you're going in there. We have ten thousand fighters there and you take charge of them. Get them ready because when that ramp goes down I want you going out. Have a full scale assault ready. While the confusion of the collapse hits them, you slaughter them. But we'll let those Romans dig and carry a while yet. They're hungry; that I know. They're getting only a trickle of supplies from the Aedui and not much from their forage parties. Caesar has two choices. He can take Avaricum and all its food or he can turn around and start for home. I'll be waiting for him if he does that. If he attacks, we'll pin them between us and our men inside. We're going to destroy him here."

* * * * *

Every day after his morning staff meeting, Caesar rode that white horse of his to where his army was working. He'd get off and walk among his men; he spoke with them and listened to them. At noon, he ate with them. Every day the disgruntled men saw his concern for them. His story was the same everywhere he went.

"There," he pointed, "is a city full of food. If you take it, everything in it is yours. But I cannot ask you to do this for me or Rome. I know you're hungry and this work is disgusting; you're Roman soldiers, not dirt diggers. And you are the best of all the Roman soldiers. We have been together a long time, but I cannot ask you to do this for me any longer. You can drop your shovels where you stand, and I'll burn those towers and we'll strike camp and go home. I am your General and you've always followed me, but this time I'm asking you to decide. Home or Avaricum?"

He knew what the answer would be. These men were soldiers and they smelled blood. They had come too far to back off now. There was more revenge to take; they hadn't had enough yet. Avaricum was full of wine, beer, and food and it was dry and warm there. There were riches in Avaricum.

* * * * *

At the next morning's meeting, Caesar looked at his generals and said, "Slaughter the mules. And any horses that we don't need for patrols."

His generals were appalled and one of the braver ones asked, "Why, Caesar, and how are we going to get our goods home if we slaughter the mules. They carry everything we have, and all the riches we've taken."

"We won't need to carry our anything home if we're lying here dead. We will be if we don't have anything to eat. My men are dying for me and the fucking mules can die for them. In case

87

you haven't noticed, and I have because I eat with them and eat like them, they are starving. The Aedui aren't delivering on their promises and there is nothing else out there. All the food in Gaul is behind that wall over there.

"I know what you're thinking. All we have to do is leave. Well, it's not that easy. Behind us a day's march away are forty thousand bloodthirsty Gauls that want nothing more than a fight with us. If we meet them we'll surely win, but how many of my men will die? Too many."

Yes, thought Brutus, too many for you to control Gaul any longer. You'd have to crawl back to Rome. The people of Rome don't like to see their war dogs in defeat.

* * * * *

An army has to carry enough food to last until it reaches a new base camp. Then local sources must provide and resupplies must follow the army. The land of the Bituriges was barren. All the grain and livestock had been hidden or destroyed or were behind the walls of Avaricum. A Roman soldier ate nearly three pounds of grain a day, with a little beef and pork or the occasional fowl. Caesar's army was feeling the squeeze of hunger. Supplies couldn't come up the rivers or travel on the roads for the Gallic patrols. Rome's allies, the Aedui, weren't helping much.

The scout rode up to Vercingetorix's tent, out of breath from the ride and the excitement of the message he brought. "The Romans are killing their livestock. Oxen, mules, horses, they're being slaughtered for the cook pots." We all laughed, it seemed a hilarious thing. But after a while I started thinking about that solitary man sitting in his tent in the Roman camp. He wasn't planning on going home.

Vercin and I rode to our hill every day. We watched the Romans and wondered what Gerromir and Quarimus were doing behind Avaricum's walls.

"We need to talk to them, Vercassive."

"No, I need to talk with them, Vercin. You need to stay here with your men rather than getting killed by a Roman outpost while crawling through some swamp! You're not a scout, nor a warrior with blood in his eye. You're the leader of all Gaul and

88

the only thing keeping these tribesmen from just riding away from this war." But he went anyway; me with him of course. We covered ourselves with mud and grass and sneaked through the marshes into Avaricum. I just hoped we could get out.

"We're digging, Vercin. We've run into nothing unusual so far, except for water seepage which is to be expected with these marshes all around us. We've got the people here helping; most of the men are too old to do much but there are thousands of carping women that we keep busy hauling dirt and timbers. We have to scrounge for the wood since we can't go outside the walls, but if need be I'll bust up the houses and furniture for our tunnel fire. It's hard to tell exactly, but I think we're moving at about the same rate the Romans are and should be under them about one hundred feet from the wall. At that point in time I can run up a signal flag and then you can give us back when you want us to light it."

"Gerromir, what's your plan?" Vercin stood looking over the wall. We were all looking down that plain. We tried to envision it how to do this. We didn't know; none of us had ever done this kind of thing before. So we boiled our plan down to this: Quarimus would signal us when the tunnel was underneath the ramp. We'd be on the hill watching for it and then make our preparations. When Vercin gave the signal, Gerromir would line up his men at the gates. Then Vercin would guess; and hope. If things worked as we planned then the Romans would see their ramp collapse and thousands of our warriors streaming through the gates at the same time. Then maybe they'd pack up and go; with our army of forty thousand waiting for them a day's march away. It would all be over in a week now, one way or the other. Our men wanted to go home too.

* * * * *

Quintus and Pexius shared their tent with six other soldiers. The eight made up the basic unit of the Roman Army, the Contubernium. They slept together, ate together, and shared the everyday utensils needed for existence. They were issued their food rations every ten days and were expected to manage that supply and cook and eat as a unit. All of this plus their axes and saws, spare pila, blankets, and the leather tent was carried by an issued mule. They also piled on booty when they took it and other things they acquired along the way. The plunder from Genabum included things for their wives or they would sell them when they returned to Narbo or Massilia, or wherever they were based. The spoils of war were why they had enlisted. The officers got the bulk of it but the men's share was considerable.

Quintus and Pexius slaughtered their mule. Every man in their Century ate some of it that night. The Century had ten Contubernium and ten mules. For the next ten days, a mule would be killed each day for each Century. Four hundred mules and horses would be killed each day for the Roman army camped outside the walls of Avaricum.

"This is a tough old fellow; I wonder how he'll taste?" Quintus didn't answer, he wasn't in the mood for talk, and the mule's blood stunk. Their grain rations were about gone and not much else was trickling in. The talk was that the Aedui were holding out; the farms and fields had been burned out when the army marched to Avaricum and the forage parties weren't finding much else. The men grumbled but they still worked. Caesar was their god of war and he'd find a way out of this.

The two men had taken their axes to the mule and clobbered him while he was grazing on some grass. They sawed off his head and hooves and hung him from a hook hanging from a tree limb. They had dropped out the stinking guts and now they were trying to figure out how to get the hide off the carcass; then would come the easy part when they cut off the meat and divided it into piles for the Century.

"I'm glad we don't have to do this every day," Pexius went on, "Secundus's unit is next, tomorrow. But maybe if they'll pay me enough I'll do it for them, now that I know how." Quintus wasn't thinking of tomorrow; he was thinking of what comes after ten more tomorrows. After the mules were gone, there was nothing left. They'd already eaten all the oxen that pulled the wagons; pretty soon there'd be nothing left to carry their possessions and plunder home.

"This pack I carry is heavy enough now; how are we going to carry that tent and the other equipment when we leave?" The soldiers sat around their fire that night. The newest soldier was from Cisalpine, Gaul and this was his first campaign.

"We'll carry it, Cellus, if we leave at all." Borros had been in the army ten years now, and he'd never seen it like this. "We better take that Gaul town over there if we're going to eat. Otherwise we won't be leaving; we'll be laying here for the birds to peck on."

The digging went on; they had to carry the dirt longer distances each day as they approached the wall. The end of the ramp was getting further and further away. There was a surprising lack of griping and grumbling, but there was a big hate building up.

* * * * *

We'd drunk a lot of captured Roman wine that night, and Vercin was gloomy. "We don't have a real plan, Cass. We just have a hope. We hope that tunnel drops their ramp. We hope that the tribesmen inside can then rush out of Avaricum and scare Caesar away; then we hope that he walks into our trap. Then we hope that we can defeat him. I wouldn't call it a plan, but it's all we've got, hope."

Brossix was there too. "We better not fight them in an open field, with their officers sitting on their horses and watching. Because when they blow those horns, things start happening that our men won't understand," Brossix mumbled back. "That's where they're best. We better keep the bastards hungry and moving along."

"I wish I knew what Caesar is planning." Vercingetorix said to no one in particular. But it gave me an idea.

* * * * *

The two Sucone warriors had been watching for two weeks now. They hid in the trees and the swamps and watched the Romans build their ramp and their towers. They knew who was in charge and who gave the orders to the ones who were in charge. One of them, a little plumper and older than the others, liked to have his privacy in the evening after eating, before going in his tent for the night. He didn't like the latrines, even the ones for the officers. His tent was near a wooded marsh and every night for two weeks, the Sucone watched him pass by the sentries and go behind a tree. The sentries knew him by now, and being an engineer favors were allowed him. They knew how long he'd be gone and he didn't go very far.

The engineer passed by them as usual that night. The sentries greeted him and allowed him through. When he was out of earshot one sentry whispered to the other, "He probably gives a good rub to something other than his ass while he's out there in the dark."

"I guess he's more bashful than you are, Cencus, I've heard you moaning and groaning unashamedly in the tent every night." Cencus swung his pilum at the other's head, and they both chuckled.

* * * * *

On the other side of the Roman camp, Quintus's *Contubernium*, the eight of them, were sitting on the ground around the cook fire, watching their evening meal boil in the iron pot. There was the usual banter about women and wine and the lack of both, and the normal griping that soldiers do about other things when a man in officer's dress appeared. He had a scarlet cloak around him and he just quietly walked up.

"May I join you for a meal?" A Roman officer stood there alone with a wisp of a smile on his face. "I hear we're having my favorite tonight, Caesar Soup. Or is it Caesar Stew? I guess that whatever you call it depends on how much of my pet gets put in the pot." The men roared and he sat down beside them; Gaius Julius Caesar the Governor of all Gaul, Senator and Consul of Rome, and Commander of the Roman Army.

* * * * *

On the other side of the camp, the engineer squatted behind a tree with a clump of leaves in his hand when the sword hilt came crashing down on his head. Then with a sack over his head and his tunic still around his ankles, he was quietly dragged into the swamp. The two men dragging and carrying him were smeared with ashes and soot to hide the paleness of their hair and skin; they had been waiting two weeks for this moment and the word they received today from Vercassivellaunus.

* * * * *

Caesar and the eight other men ate their stew. "You men have done everything I've ever asked you to do. I don't have to ask you for the next; I know your answer. Behind that wall in that rich town are the people that are eating the food that should be yours. We can turn around now and walk back to Rome or we can take that town and everything in it. Avaricum is not for Caesar, it's yours. We'll take no slaves for our officers to sell. These Gauls are going to pay for what they did to Romans here. Everything in that town is yours and when you've eaten all you want, drunk more than you need, and fucked everything in it then we'll burn it to the ground. Then we'll go home. By the way, Pexius, I hear you're turning into a pretty good butcher. Do you think you'll quit the Legion when your time is up and become one? And cut up mules for a living." The First Contubernium of the Third Century of the Second Cohort of the Tenth Legion roared; as did the nearby men who had heard of the visitor and come close to the fire. Caesar's men would follow him into fire and death itself.

* * * * *

Quarimus and Gerromir quietly passed through the marsh. They came out of a side gate and they were met by some Lemovices. The Lemovices took them through the swamps and woods to where horses were waiting to take them to Vercingetorix's camp. All of the leaders of the Gallic tribes were already there.

On the ground in front of Vercin's tent, I had laid out the situation. I knew it well enough by now; I'd been sitting on that hill watching everything for two weeks now. Yesterday the Sucones brought us a Roman captive. He talked. He wasn't a soldier, he was an old man who knew how to build roads and bridges, and he just wanted to go home to Rome. We made sure that what he told us was truthful though. There were ways to do that.

"Here's Caesar's Army, Vercingetorix, and this is Avaricum. There are marshes and rivers around the city here and here and here." I marked it all out on the ground for Vercin and the other men to see. I showed them where we were now, behind Caesar's camp a day's march away. Vercin kept staring down at my

93

marks. No one said anything, then finally "Show me where the ramp is now Quarimus, how far out has your tunnel gotten to?"

Quarimus drew a wide line in the dirt representing the end of the ramp. Then he drew two lines that started from behind the city's wall and ended at a point under the leading edge of where Caesar's ramp was. "I think we're here, Vercin. We punch holes up through the ground at the end of every day. And here and here," he pointed, "the spears found their way to air. But yesterday we couldn't punch through. I think we've reached it. That would be where the new dirt has filled the low area."

"How far can they get to by tomorrow night?" Vercin was deep in thought now. We made our plan and hoped we had guessed right. The citizens of Avaricum were to start carrying wood down into the two tunnels and pack it where we wanted the fire start. The burning wood would catch the beams and timbers that supported the tunnels. Then the fire would get to the trees thrown into the ramp. When Caesar's towers and soldiers added their weight to the ramp over where our fires had sucked out the air, the ramp would collapse.

"But," Quarimus laughed, "It's a little tricky. We have to keep the fire from getting too far along; we don't want our wall falling down too."

When the fires started in the next couple of nights, Gerromir's fighters would line up behind the main gate and the smaller side ones. As the Romans rolled their towers and engines of war down that ramp, then the earth would collapse and Gerromir would stream out of the city to face the Romans. That was our plan; or as Vercingetorix had said, our hope.

94

I have been walking the trails of this mountain for two days now. I haven't seen any sign of life other than the Roman and his whore that I had killed. I was moving quietly. It's over now and doesn't matter anymore, but I wish that Vercin had followed Draius's advice. What did it matter if we killed all the Romans or just sent them home? But that was then and now is now and we'd found the blood we wanted; just most of it was ours.

I came around a boulder this afternoon, the sun is in my eyes, and there are three Roman soldiers standing there. Two have pila pointed at me and the third has a big grin on his face. It is Gerromir. "Pardon our dress, Cass, but it's safer traveling this way."

PAT MIZELL

CHAPTER IX

Things had to be desperate now in the Roman camp; supplies weren't coming in and the foraging parties seemed to be larger and more constant in their search for grain. We had attacked and harassed them so much that they had to send more and more cavalry with them than at the start of the siege, so Vercingetorix planned an ambuscade. We'd heard that Aeneas would send one out to an area that had not been molested by them before and Vercin jumped at this chance. He'd been a general too much lately and not a warrior enough. I suspect he wanted some blood. He gathered a large force of our horsemen and left to lay for the Romans.

We always had to contend with the arguments and differences of the tribes when he wasn't there, so he left no one in charge at the main camp this time. He thought that maybe they wouldn't do anything stupid if they were arguing all the time. Caesar found out that Vercin had left and marched at midnight toward the main camp of the tribes. When he got there, he saw us on high ground with marshes around us.

We were ready for a fight, as we always were, although Caesar didn't seem so anxious. We had good position and there would have been a lot of blood let if he attacked up that hill. But this news brought Vercin back with his cavalry only to find Caesar gone. Maybe that's what Caesar intended, to look for an easy victory or too walk away if it wasn't there. But it did pull Vercin back. Some of the chieftains were furious at Vercin for leaving. When the Romans and our tribesmen stood facing each other that morning, there was the usual taunting and daring between them. They yelled at our men that Vercingetorix had left them because Caesar had offered him a separate peace and Roman support for his permanent rule of all Gaul. Our people never seemed to see how Caesar played us against the other.

Vercin sent me to bring all the important men to his tent. There were too many to meet inside, so they all gathered around us. Brossix and I stood at his back. Vercin stared at the chiefs and they started to quiet. Vercingetorix was an imposing man at any time, but when his blood was up, and it was now, he was frightening to behold, even to our savage men.

"I didn't start this war just so we could make another agreement with Rome. I started this war to drive them from our land, or kill them on it. Have you not heard Caesar's drivel before? Craustus, bring that Remi out here." The Remi were always Rome's allies; they were a Belgic tribe of us from the north who in return for helping Caesar put down the Belgae uprising, now governed that area for Rome. Their cavalry rode with Caesar's against us. As Craustus brought the tall warrior from the tent, Vercin explained.

"We destroyed a foraging party yesterday; that's what I told you I was going to do when I left this camp. I didn't go to meet with Caesar or desert you while he attacked. You knew why I had left and you agreed with me then. The reason why I didn't leave one of you in charge was because I didn't want anyone making any decisions while I was gone. I know our men are sick of just sitting here doing nothing. I know they want to go home. I know that some of you are ready for a fight. I didn't want a commander here who might succumb to that temptation. Our fight is coming but it will be on ground of our choosing at a time of our choosing.

"Remi, tell these men what you told me."

Vercin's riders had killed all the Romans of that foraging raid. He had managed to rescue the slaves that were taken along to do the reaping and working and the one Remi warrior who had had enough war and surrendered. He just wanted to go home now, so he told us of the Roman camp. We could see it from our hill but that didn't tell us what was going on inside. They were at the end, he said, of food and their own frustration. Their officers were telling the men that they would launch the attack on Avaricum in three days and then they would eat.

Vercin and I rode to our hill for one last look. We were far away but could see everything; the Roman camp, the city, the ramp that was approaching it, and the vinae that shielded their vanguard. That didn't offer much protection, just mostly limbs and leather covering, but it kept the arrows away from the diggers. It looked like there were a couple of Legions down there. A lot of them were digging and hauling but the rest guarded them from our attacks. We had attacked them constantly.

We could see the huge towers had been finished and were ready to move into position. The Romans had aboveground tunnels that were roofed and sided and would move their men into place while they waited their turns to go up the towers. When the ramp was close enough, the towers would be moved up. The Romans would fill the tunnels with men who would in turn fill the towers and when the towers' sides were lowered onto Avaricum's wall, then fifty thousand Roman soldiers would pour into the city. It was our time now.

We sent a signal to them then met Quarimus and Gerromir in the swamp that night. We were all in agreement.

"They'll attack in two days, Vercin. They're almost at the wall and we can almost spit on their vinae. Our tunnels are well underneath where the engines and towers will be placed and I've had the men enlarging them into underground caverns stacked with wood and pitch. The timbers are holding up now but we've got ventilation holes started above them and when you give the word, I'll have the men punch through and light the fires. There's enough wood in those holes to drop that ramp ten feet."

"And you, Gerromir, are we ready now?"

Gerromir nodded and told us his plan. "When Quarimus lights the fires we'll have the men ready to pour out the side gates. We'll attack the towers and turtles and any Romans in our way. We've got barrels of pitch on the top of the wall and our bowmen and spearmen there. Caesar's got two Legions down there and we can match them on the ground too."

It was a sound plan. The Romans were at the end of their wherewithal and we had a surprise for them. So Vercin gave the nod and that night it began. The Romans had finished their day's work and their evening meal and put out their sentries and patrols. The engineers were inspecting things as the towers had been moved up but most of the men were asleep. Then Quarimus started his fire.

Quarimus's miners punched through the ground above him to allow air in the caverns and then the last few of them lit the pitch and ran up the tunnels to get out of those flaming holes. The wood that had been stacked quickly caught, then the timbers that supported the tunnels, and the air from above and the tunnel entrances lit up that ramp from below. Flames were everywhere and more pitch was thrown from the city's walls. The ground started to sink. Rome's soldiers were in total confusion and then Gerromir rushed from the city's gates and attacked. Romans poured down from their camp but our archers and slingers cut loose on them from high atop the wall. It was chaos everywhere.

Vercin and I watched from the hill. Throughout that night, we saw Caesar's army deteriorate before our eyes. He eventually got everything back under control and our men retreated into the city, but Caesar's plan was in ruins. The fires burned all night and the ground continued to sink with his engines of war. His towers collapsed and were useless. The next morning, we watched as the Legions moved back to their camp a mile away. Most of them anyway.

We went back to our army, with Gerromir starting to move his forces out that night back to us. We wanted all of our men together when Caesar left. We'd be ready for battle if he wanted it; or he could just go home. That night, Gerromir's warriors started trickling in. Some of them who were from Avaricum had stayed inside the walls; their war over. There was a ferocious winter storm coming too; Caesar would have a long and wet walk home.

* * * * *

"Are there enough ladders and grappling hooks?" Caesar looked around at his generals. The grim men nodded. The wall of Avaricum had once stood eighty feet above the ground, where the ground was at its lowest. As the ramp moved up that hill, the top of the wall was much closer now. The Roman siege towers were gone, but there was still the old way. Throw up the ladders and grappling hooks and send men climbing up them. It would have been impossible before, starting from eighty feet beneath with ten thousand of Gaul's warriors firing everything they had down at them. Those men were leaving; the Roman officers could hear the women of Avaricum crying and begging them to stay. Caesar had been defeated and the men of Gaul wanted to go home.

Dicelobus spoke. "We've been hiding them under the vinae as we moved it along and added them gradually so as not to draw attention. We'll carry more as we go down there tonight, but we'll move as silently as we can. The barbarians are in their houses and their taverns telling everyone what great warriors they are and we don't want to disturb them at that."

"No," Caesar said, "Let them keep drinking and humping away by their fires. Start moving our men into place at midnight; slowly and silently. We go over at first light."

* * * * *

The people of Avaricum woke up the next morning to the sight of the Roman Legionaries standing atop Avaricum's walls. When the massacre was over that day, only eight hundred of the city of forty thousand had made it alive through the swamps to Vercingetorix's camp.

PART III

GERGOVIA

PAT MIZELL

Gerromir and the two men take me back to their camp. There are a couple of others there, but I don't know any of them. Gerromir tells me later that night that there are more in these mountains but they keep their camps small and scattered to avoid attention. Romans are still patrolling and gathering up our remnants for the slave caravans. But they aren't taking any Arverni or Aedui, just sending them to their homes.

That probably doesn't apply to me, but it doesn't matter, I am not going anywhere where I can't kill Romans. Gerromir had spied on Caesar's camp after Alesia. Vercingetorix is in a cage; and now on the way to Rome. Commius is somewhere; maybe with the Germani. Or maybe he went to Britannia, he has tribesmen there. Gerromir thinks Brossix is at his farm; Caesar's amnesty would have allowed it. And I think I know where Ladia and Vercingetorix's sons are; where I'd sent them.

We don't know what to do; only that we can't sit on that cold mountain the rest of our lives. A lot of the tribesmen from the north are sometimes friendly and even have relatives in the Germani lands across their river. Commius and some others could be there but I am not going around those tribes, they want the same thing that Rome does. Gerromir and me talk about a scout in Arvernia, but men will attract attention. There is a woman on our mountain that has was taken as a slave, but some tribesmen attacked the caravan and she escaped. But not before she killed the slave trader who had raped her. She says she isn't afraid of either anymore, so she and an old man go down that mountain. They even make it back.

CHAPTER X

The massacre at Avaricum should have devastated Gaul, but it had the opposite effect. Our people saw it was just murder. It had happened before at Genabum and other places but this time Caesar didn't have the excuse that he was putting down an insurrection like he had used at Genabum. Avaricum was just a city full of people trying to lead their lives. There weren't any of our warriors in there; they had left. Rome just climbed up those walls and then went down and murdered forty thousand people who thought their war was over.

We left. The Legions were behind the walls now with enough food to feed them through the winter. We talked among ourselves, and with the other men; all of us were sad but no one felt ashamed. We hadn't been beaten on the battlefield. In fact, Vercin had been right all along; if the people of the city had done what they said they would do, then Caesar would be pinned up on that wall right now with our army in his camp and at his back.

* * * * *

The first thing that Caesar turned his attention to was the matter of the Aedui. They had failed to keep the promise of supplying the Legions at Gergovia, and Caesar wanted answers. From Gergovia, he summoned them to come to Decetia, and they did; the old men who led the tribe and some younger ones who stood in the background. Caesar knew who they were, for Brutus had done his job well.

There was division in their people. They had laws and their own way of doing things, as most of us Gauls did, and they pick their king every year. The elders had named Cotus this year, one of the privileged of the Aedui aristocracy. A young and powerful chieftain named Convictolitanis had challenged this decision.

Brutus had determined and Caesar had concurred, that the failure of the Aedui to supply Gergovia was because of this split and he wanted a solution. Caesar didn't care who was king as long as they obeyed his wishes and could lead their people; that was the purpose of this meeting: to reestablish Roman rule. Brutus, Aeneas, and others had moved among the people of the countryside and Caesar listened, watched, and then he decided.

"Cotus, and men of the Aedui; the Roman people want nothing more than to be your allies and friends but there is an injustice here. I cannot ignore your laws any more than you can ignore the laws of Rome. Your laws clearly state that no one can rule while a member of his family who had once ruled is still alive. Your brother Valetiacus was King last year and I am at a loss as to what to say. This law, like Rome's of a similar nature, is to keep any dynasty from developing either by purpose, or by laxity caused by a casual attitude of the moment. Cotus, you are a great man and I respect you but the law is for us all to follow, and I am troubled by this all. Can you help us all here?"

Privately, once Caesar had made his selection, the elders and Cotus had stepped aside graciously, though they had no choice. Convictolitanis was now selected by the druidae and the other elders to be the new king. This was only because Convictolitanis had convinced Caesar that the others would follow him in his loyalty to Rome. He was a very powerful and influential young man. He was also a wonderful liar. Convictolitanis had been with us from the beginning.

* * * * *

The young men of the Aedui were tired of being told what to do by Rome. It was not only the young, but the farmers whose crops could only be bought by Roman merchants at Roman prices and miners and craftsmen who had their own goods to sell. The only Aedui that wanted Rome to stay were the men who made money from being Rome's representatives.

Convictolitanis and his friends had been plotting with us for months and when the time was ready, they would fight with us. And the time was almost here.

Caesar, when he thought he had the tribe under his control again, and a supply line of food from them, began his march. Convictolitanis was to bring ten thousand warriors with the supplies for the Legions' summer requirements. Caesar sent

Legate Labienus with four legions to invade the land of the Parisii. Then Caesar headed south into the land of the Arverni with the other six. We knew where he was going, and he had to get across the Allier River first.

We rode to get ahead of him, destroying the bridges as we came to them. Then we waited, but not for long. Caesar moved an army faster than anyone could imagine. They marched along one bank and we mirrored them on the other. The river was high this time of year and couldn't be forded, so we stayed opposite his army to guard against any attempt to rebuild a way across; the Roman engineers were good at that. We'd seen that before when they attacked the Helvetii.

Time was on our side; more tribes were joining our alliance, even Commius of the Belgae was making noises again. His tribes wanted Roman blood. If we could survive the summer, we felt there was a good chance that the Roman Senate would not let Caesar return next year; and he couldn't fight us in our own land during the cold and hungry time of the year that was coming soon. Caesar always seemed to find a way; or make one.

* * * * *

Rome's six legions camped in a forest by the river one night, next to where we had destroyed a main bridge. We were on the other side, watching them. When the legions left the next morning, we marched along in our dance of death. But Caesar outwitted us. He left his engineers and every third fighting man hidden in the woods. When the six legions marched out with their banners flying and their horns trumpeting we saw a complete formation and followed. We should have left scouts behind to shadow him, but we never thought of it. When the legions marched for a day and made their camp, we did the same, then the men that were left hidden behind rebuilt the bridge on the old piers. Later that night, they crossed over and built a fortified camp, while the six legions and us marched back upriver. We thought they were leaving. When we saw what had been done to us, it was too late, so Vercin turned around and rushed us to Gergovia; Caesar's goal.

It took Caesar five days to get there; we were ready for him. Gergovia was built on the tip of a ridge that faced the river with a long sloping hill and pasture land in front. We made our camps below the walls of the city, all our tribes in different areas. We could match his numbers and had the advantage of position, and help was on the way to us. Convictolitanis was marching with his men and Caesar's grain; this was our surprise for Caesar.

To our left was forest and to our right some rough land. Directly below us was a small hill on which we put some men. Caesar built his fortifications below it. The fight would be on our walls, with warriors in front of it and Romans charging uphill at them; after Gergovia every one of us was ready and spoiling for a fight. It was our turn. Caesar probed with his cavalry but the terrain was unsuited for mounted men; we had already put ours to pasture, and we waited.

Then one night they attacked our small fortress on the hill below. We had been prepared for this and withdrew our men back to the main camps; we didn't want a pitched battle that far from our walls and the hill had no strategic use to us. Around the girdle of our city was another wall of stone that marked the territory in which we wanted to fight; Roman cavalry couldn't pass it and our mounted men were inside between it and the walls of Gergovia. We had food and water and forage for our animals and the wall of the city covering our backs; and we had men who wanted war.

The Romans built a deep trench from their main camp to their camp on the small hill so they could send men back and forth from one to the other, but we could see their movements from our heights and we waited.

* * * * *

While we sat there at the city of the Arverni, the Aedui were moving. Convictolitanis's army of ten thousand was marching to Caesar's aid; or so Caesar thought. This new king put men of known loyalty to him in charge of it and depended on them to follow through with our plan. It was thus: when they reached Caesar's camp, were accepted within, and a few days had passed; upon our signal and our attack from the hill, the Aedui would rise within the Roman camp and we would destroy them.

He put this force under the noble Litavicus and his brothers, who had been with us from the start. Other than their leadership, very few of the Aedui knew of this. Most just knew that their old enemy the Arverni and their new enemy the Romans were at war. Caesar had invited a group of Aedui men to accompany him; they were his hostages, as was always the case among Gauls. Our men in this group knew to lay the groundwork for our planned attack and get word to us of Caesar's fortifications.

But treachery struck us. Among the hostages were two who Cotus and the old aristocracy had elevated through the past few years to positions of influence. When they smelled out the conspiracy, they argued over their loyalties. The one, Eporedorix, went to Caesar and told him what was going on while Viridomarus quickly alerted Litavicus's brothers who quickly fled. Eporedirix and Viridomarus were snakes. Others escaped before Caesar could react and rode to Litavicus with the news of the treachery.

When the first of the fleeing men reached him, the caravan was about thirty miles from Gergovia. Litavicus had to move quickly and he called the men together.

"Brothers, the Romans who have been telling us that they were our friends and allies have shown their true nature. They tortured some of our hostages who they had caught in contact with the Arverni, and killed them. My kinsmen are dead. Eporedorix and Viridomarus are dead. Caesar has killed all our guests in his camp and he is on his way to kill us now. They didn't ever want our friendship; they wanted us to be their servants and to use us to keep all the Keltoi from uniting. We, and the tribes we lead, are the only ones who have kept Vercingetorix and the rest of Gaul from eliminating Rome from our soil. Now we see and now we too must act."

The Aedui went wild. They killed all the Roman merchants who were in the caravan with them and immediately Litavicus set out with the supplies and his clan to join Vercingetorix, using the old routes. Vercingetorix sent Gerromir to show them the way and the passage through our patrols. Things were moving fast, though some of the Aedui who were followers of the old leaders didn't agree, or didn't believe in our cause. Caesar was moving fast too.

* * * * *

Caesar left two legions at their fortress in Gergovia under the command of Caius Fabius and told him to hold steady until he returned. Then he took the other four, leaving their heavy equipment behind, and marched in all haste to the Aedui caravan. When he got there, the Aedui who had stayed behind showed their real reason for staying; they were cowards. They fell to their knees and cried, and begged Caesar not to kill them. They said that it was Litavicus and his clan who had turned traitors to him, not them, or the Aedui back in their lands. Caesar wanted to believe that; because if it weren't the case, then he would have to admit he had made a grievous mistake in making the Aedui supreme in Gaul. He spared the caravan but took some of them back to their homeland to spread the word of the treachery of Litavicus and the generosity of Caesar.

Caesar sent Eporedorix and Viridomarus with them. "Tell your people of Litavicus's lies; show them these men. Caesar did not kill or torture them, nor the others. The Aedui are our brothers and we aren't going to harm any of you because of a few traitors. Tell your people that. Tell them not to believe those lies; but tell them that those rebels and anyone who is with them will all die at my hands."

Caesar called his Centurions together. "Our men are exhausted. I know that. They have marched thirty miles without rest and now we must go back. Vercingetorix is attacking Fabius and some Aedui are on the way there to join in. Explain to your men that Caesar and Rome calls upon them for all the strength and courage that only a Roman soldier has. Tell them that I will be at their front and marching with them. Take my horse with you and tell the men that it is theirs. Caesar walks with his men. Tell them that we rest for three hours and then we march to battle."

The men from the mountain come into camp. We send the signal and our man and woman make it and we talk into the night. There are some hard men there, but Gesataia is more full of hate and vengeance than any ten of us. Her baby had been skewered on a Roman lance and she was taken slave. But one of our patrols had ambushed the slave caravan and she'd had a taste of Roman blood; but it isn't enough yet she says. I tell her that there was plenty more to find.

Commius is up north. Litavicus is dead at the hands of his own tribe. But Brossix thinks that Teutomatos and Corsignatos have escaped, and if they have they'll be doing the same thing we are. Waiting. Winter will be here soon and the Romans will go into their camps. Caesar will parade Vercingetorix through the streets of Rome and we'll sit here thinking of our dead. And Romans who soon will be dead. But I have something to do first.

CHAPTER XI

Caesar was wrong. The Aedui were with us; almost all except for Cotus and his family and their followers. Followers of men like them are looking for riches. When those don't come, they look for others to follow. Vercin had sent men to talk to them; men who were merchants and shippers and some of the Venetti who told them of profits to be made in the island of Britannia and in the north. The Keltoi of Gaul made metal items that were wanted everywhere; and swords that Rome didn't want anywhere. They saw the riches of freedom from Rome.

We tore into the two legions that Caesar had left. The Centurion left in charge made a mistake, or Caesar did before he left. The camp was too big for the men left there to defend without stretching their lines thin, and we hit them everywhere. We had more warriors than they did and could keep sending in new bands while they had to man their walls with every man they had, and we knew that we'd wear them down. That night we rested and prepared for our victory the next day, but kept up some harassment to keep Fabius's men awake and strained. At dawn, we would overwhelm them and then wait for Caesar to come back.

"Vercingetorix, a Roman army is coming, a lot of them!" The scout was breathing heavily and obviously excited but he must be wrong; there was no other Roman army close enough to reinforce Fabius. Vercin quickly gathered his chieftains from their beds.

He told the scout, "You exaggerate; these men you saw can only be some of Caesar's cavalry. Gerromir, go see who they are and then we'll meet them with our own horse and send them back to where they came or in a pile on the ground."

When Gerromir returned, he told Vercin that it was actually Caesar's six legions. "It's him, Vercin, just two miles away. All of the fuckers." Caesar had made another miracle. Somehow, after marching the thirty miles to the Aedui, he had turned around and marched back. A prisoner that we later captured told us that a messenger had intercepted Caesar's march back and told him of the plight of Fabius's camp. Those men marched for two days up and back with barely a rest between. We should have not waited for morning.

We sat back in our camps and watched the legions march into their camp. The eagle of each of the four legions joined the two already there. The pennants and the various units stood below us. But we still had our hill and our wall and they couldn't take us. We were all camped in tribal groups between the wall of the city and the stone wall that was halfway down the hill. When the Romans came over that wall, our horse would cut them up and we'd go down the hill and finish them. All we had to do was wait for Caesar to act.

* * * * *

Caesar sat with his most trusted generals; glasses and amphorae of wine on the table and in their hands. It had been a grueling march and the men were slowly recovering while the Gauls watched and waited from their ridge top.

"We can't win here. We were lucky to survive this. If I, or any of you, had been the Gaul general, Fabius's two legions would be on a funeral pyre right now. We survived because of our discipline and the iron will of my men, and I'm not going to sacrifice them in return on a futile objective. What we will do is launch a strategic and limited attack; if we're very lucky we can rout them, but if not, we'll leave them here on their hill and take our business to the next town. We probably need to go back to the Aedui and sit on them while they get their little rebellion calmed down. Convictolanis and his family aren't going to let the people forget that the actions of a few hotheads could have caused their destruction. And if they don't see that then I'll crucify the entire leadership. Those farmers will understand that. Here's what we'll do." Caesar explained his strategy and sent them to their tents. "Staff meeting at dawn." The next morning the Legates and Centurions gathered and the plan was given.

From what we saw later and pieced together with the help of a wounded Roman, it was the usual Caesar dupe. He was good at that, but he usually could depend on the Roman legionary to follow through with a crushing savagery that made it all work. But maybe the wall of Avaricum had come too easily for them.

We faced down the ridge at the main army with the smaller hill sitting between us. We saw a few men moving from the main camp to the smaller one. To our left were woods on the side of our hill and Roman troops moved into them. Then their cavalry went around that way and we started moving our tribes to face them. We told the old men and the women in the city to be on lookout for any other forces, that their wall would hold the Romans until we came back.

It turned out that this was a ruse by Caesar. He had put helmets on his muleteers and herdsmen and with some of the standards pulled us toward the woods while he ran a larger contingent of men through his trench to the little hill. The cavalry on our left galloped around; the men in the woods blew their horns. Then the main attack came up the hill in front of the city. Without our horsemen to meet them at the stone fence, they were quickly over it and at the city's wall before we could turn around and send men back. But the women of the city saved it.

The women weren't ready to see their children massacred. They filled the top of the wall; screaming and wailing and throwing stones and boiling water down on the Romans. When they ran out of that they threw their furniture, and their clothes and jewelry and anything they had, but the jewelry and gold trinkets saved us. A few Romans, including Fabius, scaled the wall but most were too busy picking up treasure to pay attention to Caesar's horns blowing.

The feint in the woods was the first part of a three part strategy. It was meant to divert us from the main attack but Caesar knew we'd react quickly, so the main attack was the real ruse; the men in it were supposed to run down the far side of the ridge on our right chasing the attackers into where Caesar was waiting with his Tenth Legion. When we chased the attackers down, we'd hit their veterans. We'd be exhausted from our run and be crushed. But something went wrong.

The bait at their feet and the women on the wall of Gergovia made the legions deaf and blind. All they wanted was the looting and the rape that they thought was their right. We started killing them, on the wall and on the ground. Some ran, and some died and the trap was never sprung. Rome just lost a lot of men.

The next day Caesar drew his legions into battle formation. They stood in ranks all day daring us to come out and fight, but I don't think they really wanted us to. We had no reason to fight; we had won and now we just wanted them to leave Gaul. But they didn't.

* * * * *

The tribes of Gaul were together for the first time. We thought that Gergovia would be enough to make the Romans leave, but there was something we didn't understand then; Caesar had no where to go. If he left then his career would be over, and he'd see every Roman soldier in his army dead before letting that happen. Some of us wanted the same thing.

Caesar's legions marched away that day. They tried to put a brave face on but we'd beaten them and they knew it. Their lust for booty had done them in. That's what would have happened at Avaricum too if the people there had done what the women at Gergovia did. Caesar tried to make light of their retreat, but it took them five days to march from the bridge over the Allier to Gergovia, and only two to get back.

Our camp is getting bigger and that is dangerous. We try to keep the men scattered around the mountain but they always show up at the fire, where the women are; so we move. Winter is coming too. I tell Gerromir about my cave but it is too close to the shepherds' path so we go looking and find another that is over a ravine surrounded by forests. That is the only home we have now.

We want to kill some Romans, but the time is not right. We have to wait until the Legions are in their winter quarters and have forgotten about us. And we have to have food. We send Rhonda down again and she finds farmers who will help us. Since the movement of shepherds along the ranges was a usual thing people we can trust brought some sheep and grain for us and we survive.

There are rumors of fighting in the north, probably Commius. Caesar is in Rome by now and my brother is in chains. He has rewarded his soldiers well too. Each received one of our people to sell as a slave and almost a hundred thousand of us had been taken to Narbo and Massilia. And Caesar will march Vercingetorix through the streets of Rome with an iron collar around his neck; his victory parade.

PAT MIZELL

CHAPTER XII

Caesar's most trusted general, Labienus, had taken his legions to the north to attack the Parisii along the Seine River; he was in trouble too. Labienus left his baggage train with his new legions at Agendicum and marched with his four veteran ones to the town of Lutetia, which was located on an island on the river. The tribes gathered and went to meet him under an old warrior of the Aulerci named Camalugenus. He was old but he knew how to fight and he wanted Labienus, for he was the general who had tried to kill Commius by deceiving him with talk of a peace meeting. Commius never forgot, nor did any of us.

Labienus tried to get at the Parisii through a swamp but Camalugenus harassed the Romans and killed some and then the news of Gergovia got to the Legions. They heard of the defeat and the rising of the Aedui, and that Caesar was marching to the Province. Tribes were gathering all around them so the Romans wanted out. They turned south and captured a town that had boats. Most of them were across before our men could get there and a terrific battle ensued; Labienus made his escape and headed for his baggage and support troops in Agendicum. With autumn approaching, they thought they were isolated in northern Gaul with Caesar leaving Gaul and Keltoi rising around them. They were mostly right.

* * * * *

As this was going on Caesar's two puppies turned on him. Eporedirix and Viridomarus would shift like the wind all to be on the winning side. He had sent them to relieve the garrison at Noviodunum where he had stored grain and fresh horses from Spain. When they learned that the people in their great city of Bibracte had welcomed Litavicus and joined the uprising, they killed the Romans and took the Aedui hostages that were held there. By the time Caesar learned this, they were all in Bibracte and their die was cast.

Vercingetorix had trouble yet with the Aedui. Now that they had joined our war they wanted to be in charge, but the tribes met and affirmed Vercin once again. He was our leader and he would stay so.

Only Caesar knew his own true intentions; whether he was retreating to the Province or seeking Labienus, but after both wandering around Gaul, they found each other. Vercin called us all together.

"I don't know if the Romans are staying or leaving, but if they do leave Caesar will just raise more legions in the south and be back in the Spring. There's only one way to rid ourselves of him and that's to put him in the ground. This isn't between Rome and Gaul anymore; it's between Caesar and his ambition and as long as he's alive he won't return to Rome until he's destroyed us. So, we'll destroy him and then Rome is gone forever. I see no other way."

* * * * *

The Roman army was marching to Alesia and we were laying for them. We had the cavalry and Caesar didn't so we hit them and we died. Caesar had brought in German cavalry and given them fresh new horses and they chased us to Alesia after killing three thousand of our men. Some of us thought Vercin should have sent out our infantry, but he didn't. He didn't want to risk our army when we had Commius and the other tribes coming. We'd have overwhelming numbers then and all we had to do was wait, then we'd hit him from both directions and destroy his army. We sat behind the walls of Alesia and waited while Caesar dug ditches; and we waited some more.

Vercin, Quarimus, and I stood on the wall and watched the Romans. "They can dig that ditch but they're going to have to jump in it when the northerners get here," Gerromir said as he walked up. "Should I take some men and make them drop their shovels and grab their swords?"

Vercingetorix just watched as they dug. "I imagine Caesar has thought about that Gerromir, but yes, we have to slow them down. But I'm afraid it's going to just be an exercise in death." That was the first day of fifty-one that we spent in Alesia.

PART IV

ALESIA

.

Gerromir is running a race for Gesataia while I sit on this stinking mountain and see Vercingetorix sitting in a cage and Ladia wondering around a forest and I have to do something. So I'm going down. I've got some farmer's rags and it's easy enough to get dirty. I cut my hair and after a few days, I'll have a scruffy beard. Then I'll just have to act scared and meek and I'll look like everyone else left in Gaul.

It's a long walk to Nemetos, where Draius and Ladia were hiding. Most all the druidae would have come to our place of worship there in the forest. With the help of Cernunnos, the Horned One, and some handouts along the way, I'll make it, unless I meet a Roman patrol. I can carry an old hunting knife under my tunic but that's all; I might get searched and I can't fight eight horsemen anyway. I could kill one or two but that's not enough; I want a lot more than that before I leave this life. And I have to help Ladia and the boys if I can find them. They should be where we sent them, but I have to know.

Caesar rewarded his men with a slave each after Alesia. So sixty thousand of my people are walking to Rome in chains; Romans don't take the young ones, they just gut them and put them in a pile for the birds. Gerromir will start raiding soon, probably with that woman at his side and in his bed at night, but I can't sit around any longer.

I have sat on this mountain all winter, with nothing to fill my days but survival and nothing to fill my nights except the memories of those last fifty days at Alesia. We were so confident at first; we strutted around talking about killing all those Roman soldiers, going out to battle them whenever Vercingetorix turned us loose, but mostly just waiting.

Then when the hunger came with no Commius in sight, we turned those Mandubii out of the gates of their city and watched them slowly die there in front of us. That was the end of us. But we didn't know that then, during those last fifty days.

DAY 50

Alesia sat on a hill, as most of our towns did; there was a river on each side of it and high hills behind them. Between the Roman camp and us was a plain about three miles long. We had eighty thousand Keltoi warriors camped beneath the walls of Alesia with at least that many coming from the tribes. The problem was feeding an army of that size, but we laid in enough grain and cattle to last as long as we needed; thirty days was all we needed. Commius and the other kings would be here long before then. We'd then smash the legions between us.

Caesar prepared. He knew he couldn't breach our walls by coming across that plain; we had our cavalry to ride out and meet them and enough of us on the wall itself to stop any assault that survived that charge. Vercin readied and organized our warriors, organizing was always hard for us to do. He put all Alesia's foodstuff under his control; under guard. A daily ration was established for the grain but we had to slaughter the cattle and salt and dry the meat because there would be no forage for them; the pastures were to open to Roman attack. There was barely enough laid in to feed our horses, and we had to have them.

Caesar started his fortifications; we watched the line grow. Sixty thousand shovels move dirt fast and it became apparent that he meant to surround us with ditches and barricades. Gerromir then got his wish. It was a dozen miles from river to river with all the gullies and hills in between and if Caesar did surround us, there would be no way in or out. Commius was coming; all we had to do was slow the Romans down.

We attacked the workers in lightning raids but didn't accomplish very much. For every Legion digging and building walls, there were two standing in formation ready for an attack. But our men were fighting men and they wanted to fight; and we wasted a lot of blood on that plain.

Ladia and the boys came to Alesia to be with Vercingetorix. She wanted their sons to be standing by their father's side to see the final destruction of the Roman conquerors. He didn't like them traveling around and coming to Alesia, but I think deep down he was proud to have them with us. They would be kings some day with challenges of their own; a Keltoi prince needed to be blooded.

The townspeople grumbled, of course. When eighty thousand young men are moved into a town, a lot of things happen that the people who live there don't like; but that was the way it was and they would have to pay a price just like all of us were. It all was necessary. Half of our lands were already burned and thousands of us dead. We had not much sympathy for the whining and complaining that was going on. We took their food to put with ours and doled it out. That didn't sit well with them. It could be two weeks before Commius came. The tavern owners didn't complain though; nor did the young women of the town.

* * * * *

Several hundred men from the Belgae tribe of the Morini had come to us. They lived on their coast and were used to living and hunting in the swamps there. During the uprising of the Belgae a few years back, they had fought the Romans hard, for Rome was taking their trade with Britannia away from them. When the Belgae surrendered, Caesar made the Morini subject to Commius as part of the price paid to Commius to support Caesar. Labienus had tried to kill him and now Commius was on his way with his men.

Two of the Morini men came to Vercin with an idea. They said they could sneak out of Alesia at night and hide in the swampland by the rivers and spy the next day on Caesar's camp, then come back in the next night. Vercin sent them out. They were half moles anyway.

We spent the next day on the wall trying to spot them. All the men were laughing and making bets on who would see them first. Other bets were made on whether the Romans or one of us would be the first. Either way, from the wagering going on, I knew that the taverns of Alesia would do good business that next night.

About midnight that night, they came in. We could tell from the roars and laughter of the men in the camps under the wall that something had happened. Vercin, Gerromir, and I were having beer in a tavern and sent word for them to come there. They arrived, covered with slime and mud stinking to the heavens, but even so, they had a group of followers with them laughing and slamming them on their backs. When we stuck a flagon of ale under their noses, we finally got the story.

It seems that they were lying in the water on the edge of the camp earlier that night, and saw Roman officers going in and out of a big tent. They figured out from the men's behavior that it had to be the Roman officers' bath house. Since Stitius and Forcia were creatures of the swamps themselves, they had no fear of the creatures in them. When the bath house traffic subsided, they crawled around in the muck and caught some snakes, sneaked up to the tent, and threw them inside. We roared in our scorn for the mighty of Rome and we drank all night. Then the next day came.

PAT MIZELL

DAY 49

We spent a lot of time that day organizing the food supplies. Vercin was being cautious; although we had plenty, he wanted to make sure we didn't run short before our army arrived. The townspeople ate a lot and weren't used to this discipline, so they grumbled, but we finally got all of the grain under guard and our control.

Butchering the cattle was a nasty job so we did it outside the walls of Alesia. I knew that our warriors were stealing more than their fair share, but that was normal even if the townsfolk didn't like it. We were the ones doing the fighting and dying. There were about twenty thousand Mandubii in the town. They were mostly women and old men who couldn't fight. To shut them up, Vercin put them to work repairing our mail, sharpening our weapons, and hauling water and pitch to the walls, in case the Romans actually got that far. They were still a pain in the backside with their harping. They don't know what war is.

It was amazing to see the speed with which the Romans could dig. Brossix said each man in the army carried a spade and an ax as part of his equipment, and even if only a third of them were digging at any one time, twenty thousand men were making that ditch grow. Even Quarimus was impressed. I went to Vercingetorix with my concern. He was sitting in a tub with Ladia washing him and as she combed out his hair and braided it, we discussed my concerns.

"Let them dig, Cass, gives them something to do other that attack us. If they have it completed before Commius gets here, then they'll have us cut off, but our warriors aren't going to fight as one anyway. Besides, with us hitting the lines from here and the others from the other side of the ditch, we'll pin the Romans against a barrier of their own making."

I still had an uneasy feeling. Caesar knew the situation too, and if he wanted to do something, it seemed to me that we shouldn't want the same thing. I sent the Morini out again that night. They crawled around in the mud and darkness and came back before dawn with their report. At least Vercin acted more concerned when they described what they had seen.

"They're digging this ditch wide and hauling the dirt away, probably for a barricade. Looks like they're planning on staying a while; they got a lot of men working and a lot standing around protecting them."

We talked after they left. Vercin sent for Quarimus. Normally the way to overcome a barrier such as this is for the attackers to carry bundles of sticks and wood and throw them in the ditch to fill it up and give a bottom to it. Normally, a ditch has sloping sides and that makes it much easier to cross. This was going to take a lot of rubbish to fill it if we wanted to go over it; the sides of the ditch went straight down. That would mean much more to fill and make it impossible to crawl up; and there would be Roman artillery pouring down on them.

"Cass," said Vercingetorix the next day, "find some riders and send them to Bibracte and find out what's keeping the Aedui. And send Lucterios to meet the Belgae and find out when they'll be here. We need for all those to come together at one time and not just start attacking the Romans tribe by tribe; it's not going to accomplish anything unless we all hit at once and from both directions."

The townspeople were still grumbling. They said we were taking their food and giving them back barely enough on which to get by; and we were. I didn't really much care how they felt, this was a war for all of Gaul, and all of Gaul was going to have to endure it. Half of our countryside was already burned and destroyed and hundreds of thousands of our people were dead or slaves.

I kept them working. We had to have barrels of water by the walls to put out fires caused by the flaming missiles and we wanted rocks and pitch to throw down on their scaling ladders. I told the townspeople to start making bundles of sticks and to cut some poles that were at least twenty-five feet long. We could throw them together and have a bridge of sorts to go over the ditch.

With that, the cooking, and providing for eighty thousand men, the townsfolk were kept busy. That would keep their yapping down.

DAY 48

After Gergovia, my father came to Vercin and me. He had tried to keep his brother and Vercin from this war, but now he came to ask if he could help. I asked Vercin if he thought he was sincere or just wanted to keep his status after the Romans left.

"Cass, Gobanitio is a good man. His only fault is that of most men, which is to do what's best for him. He's profited from trading with Rome and he was greedy but all that have riches are so. It's our kind and those who have nothing to lose that want to go to war and change things."

Vercin put him in charge of bringing in food and supplies for the warehouses in Alesia. When Caesar and Labienus were roaming around trying to find each other, Vercin was planning a base from which to attack them. This hilltop town was the best location. We had been bringing in grain and other foodstuffs for weeks now, and added to them the stores of the local Mandubii.

"Boys," he still called us, "you told me to put in enough food for sixty thousand men to last thirty days. I've had all the chieftains count their tribesmen and that's about the number. But, riders and small groups of them are coming in every day from all over Gaul and I don't know how many we have now. The twenty or so thousand people of Alesia had their own harvests, which were plentiful but refugees are arriving from the countryside and they aren't bringing much with them. We could have as many as a hundred thousand people to feed."

We walked through the warehouses as we talked. "Each of those barrels over there will hold about four hundred pounds of grain. Brossix says that the Roman soldier is rationed at three pounds per man daily. Taking into account that a lot of those people are women and children and our men aren't marching everyday we shouldn't need as much, but still, men are fighting and the people are working and it takes a lot to keep the belly full.

"I would say that each person here needs about two pounds of grain per day. That, with the peas and turnips, should be enough. We've slaughtered over two thousand cattle and some pigs and are working to salt them away now. But a lot of them became feasts the night the soldiers saw them being butchered."

We walked from building to building and Father counted as we went. "So it takes five hundred barrels of wheat and barley a day to keep this mob alive. If you figure an ounce or two of salted beef or pork a day per person that's about ten thousand pounds a day. We're salting that away as fast as we can because every day an animal is alive we have to feed it grain, they don't have any pastures to graze now. There are a lot of peas, carrots, turnips, onions, and that sort of thing in storage, but we have to keep some cattle and goats alive to provide milk for the children.

"We have eight thousand barrels of wheat, about two thousand of millet, and a couple of thousand of barley. If you consider that which the livestock and horses must have we've about half what we need to last thirty days. So many people have arrived without much but what's on their backs. We need those wagons rolling in with more food."

The problem was the wagons couldn't roll in; the German cavalry were roaming the roads and killing everybody and everything that moved. The Aedui hadn't yet come, nor their promised supplies.

"But the biggest problem you have, Vercin, is the twenty thousand horses here now. They can't pasture much and they eat a lot of what we do, even if it is inferior grain. The good thing I can tell you is that we've got enough beer here to last a year."

Vercin looked at me and said, "I don't know if that's good or not, but let's go get rid of some of it."

We went by Brossix's station and sent for Sedullos and the others to meet us that afternoon. There were twenty-four tribes represented at Alesia, and they all had their opinions of how to wage this war.

Vercin finally let out a shout. "Shut up the arguing, you're starting to sound like a bunch of old women. Everyone has his say and we'll take all that is in account. This is not Arverni or Limovicum or Moriniam or anywhere; this is Gaul! We will fight as one and speak with one voice. Drink some more of that fucking beer and act civilized." Everyday it was like that. That changed soon enough when we started fighting Romans again.

PAT MIZELL

DAY 47

Our spies went out every night, but we could stand on the walls and see the progress the Romans were making. Quarimus was keeping a tally and he figured that in another week the big trench would reach from river to river.

We hit them as they came across the field carrying their shovels and buckets. Two thousand Arverni rode with me out of the gate, but before we could even approach the workers, the Roman cavalry were on us. Caesar must have hidden them there in the trees by the rivers between the times our spies came in and dawn. They came from both directions just as we reached the gap between the end of the trench and a river; we were stuck in the middle of the two fangs and paid for it.

The fighting was awful; we had Romans on each side of us throwing their pila. When we finally got organized, the Roman infantry was pouring across the meadows. We killed a lot of Romans. We were savage animals that day, but a lot of us were dead when the day was over. Vercingetorix tried to get a relief force to us but they were slow and the Romans weren't. For the first time in a long time, we felt the might of the Legions. We were like screaming, clawing, spitting children to them and they chewed us up.

By the time we made it back to the gate, all of the men outside our wall were scrambling to get inside. All of our horses and warriors were stuck trying to get in with the Romans and Germans killing us from behind. Most of us got in but some didn't and most of our horse herd was driven off or captured. Vercin closed the main gate, but all morning our men were climbing the walls and dying on them. We learned something that day; our fury couldn't match the discipline of the Romans, and I'm not sure if our leaders could match Caesar. He was a soldier and we were just warriors, and there is a difference.

We sat in the house in which Vercin was staying with Quarimus and Brossix. Gerromir was trying to put back together the pieces of our army and our shattered morale. "That trench is twenty feet deep, Vercin, and it looks like Caesar means to have it all the way across the field." We had our own trench, dug before the Romans arrived, and we even had a stone wall behind it six feet high. We were still surprised by Caesar's plan.

Vercin answered, "I thought he'd come straight at us with his siege engines and artillery; but he's trying to keep us in Alesia, not pull us out. What does he think he's doing? We can just sit here and wait for the others to come."

No one answered Vercin for a minute or so, then Brossix finally spoke up. "The man knows what he's doing Vercin, he's not stupid. If he's doing something, it's because he wants to not because he doesn't know what else to do."

"Yes, Bross, but does he think we're just sitting here? Doesn't he realize he's in the middle of Gaul with sixty thousand of his men that have to be fed every day and our people gathering to smash him?"

"Getting back to his fortifications, Vercin, that ditch is not only twenty feet wide but it's twenty feet deep, and the unusual thing is that the walls of it are perpendicular, there won't be any climbing up the other side. It's going to take ladders or bridges to get at them." No one looked at Quarimus but we all knew what that meant. We'd have thousands of pila raining down on us while we were trying to get out of it, and then when we did, if we did, the Germani and Roman riders would be all over us.

Vercin was confident. "We aren't going to respond to his invitation. We're going to sit here, slow down his efforts and when Commius and the Aedui come, we'll fight him then. Time and numbers are on our side. If that bastard wants to stay in Gaul then we'll let him; he can spend eternity in one of his own ditches."

Brossix didn't say anything, but I was looking at him while Vercin talked. He looked like he was about to pop; his face was red and steaming when we left together that afternoon. "He's not stupid, Cass."

DAY 46

Caesar strode into the command tent. His generals were gathered. "Good morning gentlemen; I trust you all slept well. Did everyone enjoy their baths last night?" Labienus laughed at Caesar's remark. "I think Aeneas's mentula will be drawn up forever, Caesar; you should have seen him flying naked out that bath house." The group of officers roared, including young Aeneas, but that night the snake had scared him out of his wits.

Caesar's attendants served a breakfast of toasted bread and cheese and some excellent but very watered down wine. When the generals were finished, the Greek slaves cleared the table and Caesar began his meeting.

"Status; cavalry first, Antonius."

"Each Legion's complement is almost full, Caesar, plus about five thousand of the Remi and Urdus's Germans to ride for us. All are reasonably mounted and we have plenty of pasturage and forage available. None of the Gauls is roaming about either. They're lying around roasting and eating their cows. We're at top condition."

"What's their attitude? Are they a ready to fight?"

"Yes, Caesar. The Germani ignited a fire in them it seems, something did. Our men are in a vicious mood now."

"Labienus."

"We're rotating the duties, Caesar. Twenty thousand are digging while twenty thousand are on guard or on alert; the other twenty rest. Each day they'll shift; they're eating well and in good spirits in spite of the labor. I think the loot they got after Avaricum has them looking more favorably at the barricade work now. Knowing what will follow."

"Egius, what is the status of the defensive works? When will the main trench be completed? You noticed I said 'main trench' because I want two more after that. Those two are to be closer to our ramparts. How is the timber situation, do you have enough?" Aeneas sneaked a look at his friend Trebonies, a hint of a smile in the look. Caesar was long regarded by his men as a genius at engineering works and his ever present attention to detail.

"Plenty of trees, Caesar, we just have to cut them and move them."

"Well, put the slaves and muleteers to work there if you need them. The Legions can wait on themselves, but get that wall started," Caesar waved his arm and the meeting was over.

* * * * *

Every Roman soldier carried a shovel, either on his person when on a march or patrol, or on the mules when the baggage train was with them. Every night, they dug a trench around their camp and built a barricade. Every morning, when they moved on, they tore that down and filled back up the trench; they were used to the digging and they had learned the value of the defensive preparations many times over. They didn't mind the work any more, for they knew they were protected while they waited for the inevitable assault.

The Gauls had a trench of their own, and a wall of piled stones behind it. The Roman engineers directing the massive trench just laughed at the paltry excuse of a Gallic barricade. The Roman trench grew quickly along a line from the river on one side of Alesia to the banks of the other on the other side. There was only one interruption in it when it was finished; a rugged hill was near one end and it was mostly rock. The area around it was laced with ravines and rock formations, so the engineers built dirt walls and barricades there; they thought that would do.

* * * * *

Back in Alesia, I went looking for Vercin. I wanted to take the Arverni out. He and I walked and found a shaded spot where we could sit and talk. "I think an all out raid, Vercin. The few thousand of us who have good horses, anyway. We need to bleed the Romans some and our men need to get over the other day. Our tribesmen will listen to me and stay as a group. I want to hit Caesar hard and let him know that this is no easy thing he's started. And I want his men to see their own blood and realize that death can come to them too."

"When?"

"We'll be mounted and ready by first light. When dawn breaks, we'll go out all the gates at once. A fast trot and then the gallop when we get past our ditch and wall. We've got the crossings over them marked and can get through them quickly enough. The Romans should be reaching their ditch about the time we start the charge. They'll have the Centuries with them but maybe not their cavalry. The Germans like to get over their drunkenness before they fight in the morning."

So I made ready. We gathered behind the gates that night and slept there. I didn't want the usual confusion in the morning; and at the first appearance of light in the east, I gave the shout and the guards opened the gates.

DAY 45

We cantered our horses through the five gates on the front and the sides of Alesia, then quickly assembled into a line and moved out in a trot. At the stone wall, we slowed and went through the openings that had been made for us the night before, then went over the wooden planks that had been laid across our trench. We moved into a line; there were over two thousand of us Arverni; then we charged at the Romans who were just now reaching the end of their trench.

We hurt them badly. My men were disciplined and angry; they had been sitting around too long watching our people getting their asses kicked; we cut down over a hundred Romans in our first charge. As we turned, we saw the Remi horse coming out of their camp but we made another pass through the lines of the Roman infantry anyway, and then we turned to face their cavalry. There was no fear in the Arverni that morning and I think the Romans were surprised at our cohesiveness. You can see when fear comes to your enemy; it's in their eyes and in their actions and when the Germani finally arrived, we were ready for them too. We had been fighting those bastards for a long time and they didn't intimidate us either. It was a good slaughter. The Arverni rode back through the gates of Alesia with their heads high and the blood of their enemies on their arms.

* * * * *

Marcus Antonius sat on his horse shaking in anger as his officers rode up. "You fought like women, no, not even women. You fought like cowards. Get out of my sight. All of you put your men in formation, then come to my tent. Your day is just beginning." He turned his horse from his officers assembled on the battlefield, and rode through the dead men and the screaming dying horses to give his report to Caesar. Caesar just glared at Antonius. When Caesar was at his angriest, he couldn't speak. He just stared at his commander of horse. Finally, he turned and walked away.

* * * * *

Brossix was working at a forge, he was hot and sweating, and so was the metal he was hammering on. "Bross, it's too late to arm sixty thousand men. If they don't have swords by now we're in trouble!"

He grinned at me in greeting. Mirandia saw me and brought me a glass of wine; it seems the Roman merchants in Alesia had left a good supply behind in their haste to leave last month. He wiped his face, got his cup and the amphora, and we went to talk under the shed.

"You've been quiet, my old friend, what is troubling you?"

"Everything, Cass. I don't like being the cheese in the trap. The rat is just sitting out there licking his chops; everything Caesar does is cold and calculated and don't think that he doesn't know what we know. He knows what we know and some things we don't."

"There's not much we can do if that's the case, Bross. We can only go with what we're given. Soon, we won't even be able to walk away if we want to, and Vercin's not going to surrender. At the very most, he'll let Caesar leave if he'll go back to Rome, but he really wants to kill them all. I'm just afraid that even if we destroy the Legions it'll just infuriate Rome and they'll return with more armies than ever.

"Draius says that the Senate would try with draw him, but if Caesar doesn't agree then they'd have to take his charter from him and he's too popular with the people for that to happen."

"Have you seen Draius, Cass?"

"Yes, we've talked. I'm always in contact with him, sometimes in ways you wouldn't understand."

Brossix laughed, "I forget sometimes that you're of the druidae, Cass. Do you miss that life? Or are you a warrior forever? Me, I just want to take my wife and go home and build my tools and arms again. I've killed enough for one lifetime and who knows who or what I'll be doing in my next one."

"You'll probably be a goat, you already smell like one."

* * * * *

At a little village about a two hour ride away, Urdus and some of his Germani were setting fire to the buildings of the town. Some of the Germani were. The screams from some of the

146

houses meant some were busy with other things. There were dead boys all about the yards; a few old men were dead too, mostly lying in front of the doorways of the homes. Urdus watched his men fill the wagons they had found; furniture, cooking utensils, a few clothes that weren't bloodstained, and what food and drink they could find.

The screams would be left behind; in fact, they soon stopped and the Germans rode away.

* * * * *

Caesar stood in front of his tent and watched the plumes of smoke all around the horizon. He and every man in the camp knew what they meant. Wars were brutal and vicious, but the Germani made it worse than that. Caesar had seen their leftovers too many times before. He turned to a slave and said, "Wash my tent in the morning." Caesar went into his room and pulled the curtain.

DAY 44

Commius, the king of the Atrebates and self-appointed war chief of the Belgae tribes, was furious. He had promised two hundred and fifty thousand warriors to Vercingetorix and he couldn't even get the kings of the other tribes to meet with him. The Morini, he could understand. After the uprising a few years before, Caesar gave the rule of them to Commius, as a reward for ending the rebellion. But that was in the past now; other than collect taxes from them, he left them alone.

The Nervii were another story. They hated the Romans and Caesar in particular but still ignored Commius's call for war. Why, was the question; and why were the other tribes waiting for the Nervii? Commius dressed in his finest clothes, fine Roman clothes that he had found in a recent raid on a Roman merchant's caravan, called his personal bodyguard of five hundred of the finest Attrebate warriors, and went to the Nervii lands.

The Atrebates arrived at sunset, and they were greeted warmly by King Boduognados of the Nervii. He had a feast prepared for Commius and the more important of his men; a freshly killed boar was roasting on a bed of coals. They went into the King's house to wash themselves and to prepare for the evening meal and the normal rounds of drinking that went with it. All of the swords and knives were left outside the door; Belgae men knew better than to mix ale and tempers with sharp edged weapons.

Commius had brought a special treat with him. The same caravan that furnished his new clothes contained a dozen or so amphorae of the best Italian wine, from the farms of the Keltoi who lived in the Po Valley. After the thanks to The Horned One and salutes to the warriors of Gaul, Commius spoke to Boduognados with all the assembled men listening carefully.

"It's past time to go to the south, my friend. I've promised the Gauls we would fight with them and now they have Caesar cornered and need us to smash him out of Gaul and Belgae forever." Boduognados was pulling a chicken apart as he listened to Commius. Finally, he washed his hands from a nearby bowl of water, took a large drink of the Cisalpine wine, and looked into Commius's eyes. It was an angry look and the room was suddenly very quiet as all turned to this conversation.

"Commius, my old friend, we have known each other a long time. We have hunted together, feasted together, and made war together. Our tribes have held each other in their arms and bled together. We have always had the same enemies and been friends with each other. We have the fucking Germani constantly raiding our towns and killing our people. Sometimes the Gauls make war on us; but this new enemy, Rome, is different.

"When they chased the Helvetii down and destroyed them, we all rose together. We know that Rome wants us to be their slaves; we, all the tribes of Belgae, were united in our attacks on the Legions, but the Remi turned on us. They liked the promises that Caesar made to them. But we warred, you and I, we didn't care for the Roman promises. They had promised the Helvetii to protect them from the Germani, and they didn't. When the entire nation finally had enough and attempted to move west to better lands, Caesar tracked them like they were animals. And when that great people had enough and turned to do battle Caesar destroyed their army. But even that wasn't enough. He chased down and killed the women and the children, and only fifty thousand or so of a nation of two hundred and fifty thousand escaped back to their old homelands.

"This is how Rome treats her friends? Caesar told us he would help us fight the Germani and keep them out of our lands; yet he has sent for them to help him destroy the Arverni at Alesia. Thousands of the murderous Germans are killing Gauls right now there. What has Caesar promised them?

"After Caesar defeated us several years ago he told us that we would be friends of Rome; he would build us roads and bridges and send the good wine and the civilization of the Roman way of life to us. He has. He built those roads. And they are full of Roman merchants taking the things we make and farm and build away from us at the prices they want to pay us.

150

Caesar has destroyed the Venetii and the other coastal people. We can't even trade with Britannia now. Everything goes down those roads to Rome, including thousands of slaves who were once people of Belgae and Gaul.

"Yet you went with Caesar to conquer the Britains; you made war on our cousins for Caesar. You were given the rule of the Morini by Caesar and you have treated them harshly and taken away their living. And now you want to lead my men into your war with Caesar? Why do you want to do this war? I don't think it is to help our brothers in Gaul; I think it's because Caesar turned on you like he has done to all of us at one time or another.

"When we first made war on the Romans six years ago you knew what their intent was, and you fought with us, no man was more fierce than Commius, nor more valorous. But Caesar seduced you; what would make me think that he couldn't again? I know Labienus tried to have you killed. And I know that Caesar disavowed any complicity in that. Do you believe him? Can the Nervii put our lives in the hands of Commius? The same Commius that didn't ride with us, but with Caesar? Tell me, my old friend, of why I'm wrong about this."

Every man in the room had listened to this. Commius had not said a word but the blood vessels on his forehead were about to burst and his eyes were fairly glowing in anger and embarrassment. Boduognados had not raised his voice when he spoke; he just talked as if he was telling another hunting story to tell a group of friends. Words like this made men kill and might yet again. There were five hundred Atrebate warriors in a city of a thirty thousand Nervii. Boduognados spoke again when Commius remained silent.

"I know these aren't the words you want to hear, but they are true words and are what the other Belgae tribes feel, too. My men can go with you if they want to, I won't stop them. But I will not lead them into a war where there is so much distrust among us. Enjoy my hospitality, my old friend, and leave us in peace tomorrow. All of us who wish to go with you will be ready at dawn."

151

DAY 43

The huge trench was almost complete. It stretched from the River Ose to the River Oserain, over ten miles long. A tremendous amount of dirt comes from a hole that is twenty feet deep and twenty feet wide and has a breadth of ten miles, and all of it had been carried to build a Roman wall four hundred feet away. That wall would stretch for fourteen miles and would stand over twenty feet high and there would be sixty thousand Roman soldiers behind it with ballista and scorpio to throw their heavy spears and rocks into anyone attempting to cross that plain; for over three hundred feet our attackers would be under a barrage. That was after they had crossed the huge trench and endured these missiles. Then they would face sixty thousand of the greatest fighting men in the world.

Caesar stood on the hill in the area that couldn't be joined with the main defense fortifications and watched the work continue. "Egius, how about this hill we're standing on. How do I defend it with no trench?"

"It's solid rock underneath that inch of soil, Caesar. We'll build a barricade here and have extra towers for your men. If the Gauls try to attack us here they'll find it's just a killing ground and they're in the tip of a funnel they can't get out of."

Caesar walked the ground; his scribe was writing as fast as Caesar talked. Caesar was at his best when he had a challenge like this and he was vibrant as he made his plans. "Will you finish tomorrow?"

"Yes, my general, there'll be some tidying up to do and some more dirt to haul away but yes, for all practical purposes we'll be through tomorrow."

"Come to my tent tonight and we'll make some plans for this hill. I want it locked down tight."

* * * * *

"I just walked by Caesar's tent and all of the engineers are going in carrying more of their models. I guess they're dreaming up more digging for us. I thought when this ditch was finished we could rest and get ready for a fight," Pexius told his tent mates. Cellus, the newest man, was stirring the stew while the bread baked and the other men except for one were cleaning their tunics and selves; they had been digging all day and would rotate to guard duty tomorrow. They would have to be spotless.

"You have been with Caesar long enough by now to know that the work is never done, but remember, it's to keep us safe, so shut up your complaining." Quintus was the senior of the eight, having eight years in the Legion. He had started in Hispania and fought his way through there and now Gaul. He had seen the young pups come and go; they came with dreams of glory and riches and usually left in a pyre of ash and smoke. Nevertheless, they were comrades; they ate together, fought together, slept together, and sometimes complained together. The eighth man came into the firelight.

His name was Therus, the only Italian in the squad. There were all Romans, but some were from Hispania and others from the Transalpine and Cisalpine. Therus had lived in Rome and he was a thief. That night he was their thief.

"I lifted this fine ham out of the officers' wagon, no porridge for us tonight! Who's buying the wine?" The seven men delightedly and quickly formed a collection of silver while Pexius scampered off to the makeshift tavern area that always followed the Legions. The man of the hour sat down and took off his armor.

"How did you do it, Therus? They watch those wagons like hawks."

"Yes, but these hawks tonight were watching the sky. Smoke is coming up all around us a few miles away. I guess the Germans are having one of their special kind of festivals tonight; the one where they kill everybody and burn their houses. I snuck up under the wagon closest to the latrine and just traveled underneath the other ones until I could smell meat instead of shit; I wish I could have found a cheese too."

"You did wonderful. Now we've got to figure out a way to roast it so the other squads don't smell it cooking. How about if we dig a hole and cover the ham with coals?" The legionary, Roz, who had come from a wild area of Hispania, knew these things. He had lived in enough camps in those remote mountains that he could cook a snake with a moonbeam.

They sat around their fire, late into the night. They were full of pork and bread, and a considerable amount of rough wine before they ran out of it and got into the raw beer that the Gauls made.

"I'm going to have one of the young ones when we take that town. One so young, she doesn't even have tits."

"Shut up Rounia, I don't like to hear that kind of talk."

"You shouldn't be so pious, Quintus, you have your share of cunnus, too."

"That's a soldier's right, Rounia, but you don't have to fuck the children."

"So what's the difference, we kill them anyway." Rounia went into the tent.

* * * * *

Caesar studied the terrain of Alesia represented by the plaster model on his table. It showed the town on the hilltop, the Gaul's stone wall beneath it, and their ditch. Then toward the Roman camp, there was the huge trench that had just been finished. The dirt from it had been carried by mule and oxen to a line four hundred feet away where an almost insurmountable wall enclosed the Roman camp. There were some cavalry postings outside of it, but they would be on the outside anyway when the fighting started.

Caesar's staff meeting started with him in giving his new orders. "Put a turret every eighty feet, Egius. I want them big enough to hold a Century each supporting each one. Twenty-four hours a day. That means I want two thousand men standing and alert at all times. Each one will have ballistae or a scorpio and a stockpile of missiles up top and more below. Ten thousand men will be working on the fortifications each day while another ten thousand are in formation guarding them. I don't want any more surprises like the one the other day."

"Labienus, see to the organization of the men. Egius, put stakes on top of the wall and point them in all directions like a porcupine; make them sharp and long. Finish my wall and get that hill fortified; I've got more ideas to start on. Two days, I

155

want it done, then report back here. Leave some of that plaster you use." Caesar waved as he turned at walked to his private quarters.

DAY 42

We could see the progress of the trench; it was almost completed now. Vercin started night attacks but those didn't do too much good. Rome just kept digging. They had piled the dirt from it into a barricade that ran the width of the plain. They were cutting trees and bringing them there to erect in the dirt mound. Wagon after wagon rolled into the Roman camp full of trees and timber beams.

We sent our spies out again to find out what was going on. You don't need to have trim trees for a barricade. The Morini came back and said that the Romans were assembling them into siege engines. It was curious. Were they planning an assault after all? They used battering rams and huge catapults to assault a town, trying to knock down the walls and gates. They would be under constant attack from our horse if they tried to move those engines across that plain.

Gerromir led a raid last night on the Roman cavalry camp nearest the river on our left. It was bloody, like all of them were, but we held our own. Our horses were getting more and more shot every day. The pasture for them was eaten down and we didn't have enough grain to give them much. Grass will only sustain a horse for so long; they need oats and barley for strength. We mostly waited behind our wall and attempted to shoo away the Germans that tried to cross our ditch and stone wall.

* * * * *

"Egius, this is what I want. The Celts have their little trench and stone wall, they'll cross it easy enough to come to our big one. They'll have a hard time filling and crossing it; my ballistae are aimed at it and when they do, they'll be mowed down. But, some will make it. So we will dig two more between it and our barricade when the wall is finished."

"That will be in two days, Caesar. It'll be fifteen feet high with the wooden stakes extending it even higher. Men are cutting trees and bringing them in now."

"What of my siege engines?"

"Arriving sir, and being assembled. I have an engineer attached to each of the twenty three towers and he is supervising the assembly and placement."

"I want the towers with two levels, Egius, each of the two with ballistae on it. And scorpio also."

* * * * *

The Roman siege engines were descended from the Greeks. They weren't a lot different but Caesar had taken their use to new levels. Normally, the Roman army attacked a town and used their catapults to throw huge rocks at the town's gate and walls to weaken them, and then a tortoise would be built leading to the front gate. The tortoise was a wooden shell that protected the men within from missiles while they battered the gate with a huge ram. Other smaller ballista rained arrows and rocks at the enemy on top of their wall. Caesar was very much a believer in anything that could save his men's lives, and very innovative in his use of machines and engines.

At Alesia, there would be no Roman attack, so the great siege engines were used in a defensive manner. The ballistae resembled a gigantic crossbow and used the same kind of torsion to drive a missile for great distances. Caesar had developed a new twist. They still threw the great rocks at distances but when men approached, baskets were attached to the arm of the machine and were filled with small rocks and pieces of metal that would send hundreds of man-killers at the attackers.

There was a smaller engine called a scorpio. It could be used with one a man or two in attendance and fired arrows as fast as it could be loaded, which was quick. The scorpio were easy to assemble and move. Caesar shifted them to wherever the action required. Hundreds of them were assembled and placed on Caesar's wall and in his towers and huge mounds of arrows were stacked nearby. Two men could move and shift the scorpio and keep a continuous hail of arrows going while a third constantly resupplied the arrows.

The engines were built in Rome and the provincial towns and then transported in unassembled pieces to wherever the Roman legions needed them. Once the wagons of parts arrived, the engineers easily put them together. The engineers could also build new ones from trees if they needed more. There were hundreds of ballistae and scorpio on or behind the Roman barricades, pointed at the trenches the Gauls would have to cross. And the four hundred feet of plain that brought them to the Roman lines. That ten mile long, four hundred foot wide stretch was a killing field.

PAT MIZELL

DAY 41

All the kings and war chiefs met that morning. Vercin had sent for us.

"Our horse is accomplishing nothing now; it can't within the confines that the Romans have established. They're just eating and shitting all over the place. We don't have enough food to keep them alive, or even us at this rate. Sedullos, I want you to take the cavalry out of Alesia. Get out of here while you can still get past the Roman lines. Take all the men of the tribes that are on horse and ride to our towns. Tell them I need every man that can shoot a bow or sling a rock to come to Alesia.

"We're going to have to attack the Roman camp; if we sit here we'll run out of grain. The townspeople are angry and starting to resent our warriors being here; they don't think of them as "our warriors" yet. Their asses aren't in danger yet. Commius is supposed to be coming with two hundred and fifty thousand men, but there is no sight of him. Ride away, get every man who can fight and tell them I need them here or we all die. Then get back and stay in the hills until Commius arrives and then we'll destroy Caesar for good. Tell the people of your lands that Vercingetorix needs them; tell them that Gaul needs them. Then we will kill Rome forever."

Brossix and I walked to his house and Mirandia fed us some fresh bread and cold venison that she had bought at the market; it would probably be the last we'd see. Then I sat and watched Brossix working on his metals.

"I'm making swords for Vercin's boys. Little Celtillus and Gobitio will be warriors in a few years and must learn the way of the warrior."

"Come on, Bross, they're eight years old!"

"We may not be here to help them for long, Cass, and I want them to remember me, and Alesia."

Brossix hammered the little swords, and heated them again, and then hammered them some more. "Every warrior in the world wants our swords, Cass. The Greeks don't have metal and even the lands that do can't make ones like we can. It's all in the process. You can take the iron ore and heat it easy enough, but that's not enough. The Keltoi in Britannia make swords but they just bend in battle. The Romans make a reasonably good sword, but not like ours. And of course the Germani just want to beat you to death with axes and clubs so they don't care. But the Greeks appreciated our work; now though the Romans won't let our craftsmanship be traded; unless it's to them. And I'm not working for any fucking Roman. Thirteen years with them was enough. Those arrogant prissy sons of senators think they are the gifts of the gods to the world and half of them don't even know which is the sharp side of a weapon." I thought to myself that some of them must, they've sure killed enough of us.

"I melt the iron, and take a piece while it's hot and hammer it down. Then I take this other ore and heat it and the iron again and then hammer them into one piece all beat together now. Then I do the same thing all over again and keep hammering them. This makes the iron hard; our people have been doing it this way since we came to these lands. Not every land has the ores we do and none of them knows our technique. If you don't put enough with the iron, then it will bend. But if you put too much of this ore with it the sword becomes too hard and it will break. We do it and get the right hardness and flexibility.

"This bar is the same length that our men's swords are made from, but after a few more heatings and hammerings I'll cut it in half and shape them. When they're finished, I'll put a good edge on them, not too sharp, they are little fellows still. The boys will then have swords that they can handle, but the same quality of a man's."

That night, Sedullos and the horsemen started trickling out. It took them all night, but the eleven thousand or so warriors were gone by morning. That was twenty two thousand fewer mouths to feed in Alesia now.

DAY 40

"Finish, Egius. There is more to do yet." Caesar had been awakened by the officer on watch when the Gauls started riding out of Alesia the previous evening. He had watched and said nothing to anyone. Just watched them go.

"Caesar, the nearest of the new ditches are in low ground. Water is seeping up from the bottom and I think we can open up the river banks and fill it with water."

"How long?"

"Just a few hours."

Caesar walked the room and thought. "Put stakes in the bottom before you let the water in."

That night Marcus Antonius, Labienus, and some others were in the baths at the same time. It was part of a Roman officer's daily ritual. The leather bath tents were carried everywhere and were put up once the officers' sleeping tents were erected. Each had several glazed tubs that could hold water that was heated by large stones. When the stones weren't being used for warming the water, they were put in the fires again then stacked in a separate part of the tent. This area had benches where the officers could lie and sweat before they got in the water. Greek slaves kept this whole process going, and after the men had enjoyed their sweat and soak, then they were dried and oiled by these Greeks. Then they scraped the officers down with curved bones, removing the oil and last residue of dirt and sweat.

"Labienus, this is my first defensive battle. When I was with Gabinius in Syria we always attacked." Marcus Antonius was from an influential Roman family, as was Labienus, but Titus Labienus was a fighting general of many wars with Caesar in Hispania and Gaul.

"Caesar likes to attack and the plain is a good battlefield for the legions, but the Gauls have the numbers, Antonius. We could win but a lot of good men would die. Instead, we'll let Gauls die on our walls this time. When they cross those trenches, they'll be

163

under a constant barrage from our ballistae. They have three to cross, not counting their own, and there'll be little surprises for them along the way once they do. Caesar has men sneaking out at night planting iron hooks in the ground and little pits that they put sharpened stakes in, then cover them with limbs and such. When they cross the last trench, those that are left, anyway will be bunched up.

"As they get closer and more bunched, the men on the towers and walls will shift the ballistae to point toward the middle of the attack, wherever it's the heaviest. That way, the rocks and darts will be moving through the Gauls line; if they miss, they just keep flying and rolling along and through the Gaul attackers.

"Then, when they get close, the artillery men will push the ballistae aside and bring in hundreds of scorpio. They're loaded fast and furious and the Gauls will have a hailstorm of arrows on them. The scorpio are easy to move around and our men will shift and move them to where ever the attack is concentrated. If we're lucky, and things follow normal, we'll dictate that concentration by our missiles and then as the Gauls hit the wall we'll loose our pila on them.

"The savages that make it past all of that will throw up their ladders and ropes and scale our wall. When they get to the top Roman legionaries with swords will be waiting for them. No one beats a legionary with a sword. There, on that wall, they'll die."

* * * * *

The great men of Gaul were riding. Sedullos, the war chief of the Lemovices rode with his tribesmen. It was good to be on a horse and not have a German or Roman cavalryman in his face. They rode hard and far; they had to find more men for Vercingetorix. In the north, Commius was gathering the warriors who would ride with him to Alesia. He had been to all the tribes, and now he was back at the town of the Nervii.

"King Boduognados, my friend, I ask to speak to your men." Commius had been in a fury for the past week. He had ridden to all the other tribes and addressed their Kings and was now back to speak with the Nervii.

"I must say this. I did ally with Rome after our war; we were beaten and the Atrebates had to survive. And yes, I was given rule over the Morini, but I treated them better than a Roman army would have. Caesar told me he wanted to control the Belgae trade with Britannia; that he was going to conquer it and we would rule there. The Atrebates have kinsmen there. Part of our tribe moved there long ago and they weren't welcomed by the Keltoi who lived there already. All we wanted was land to farm and live on but we were attacked and spit on; I have no love for Britannia. We must live, and it's better to have slaves than it is to be slaves.

"I went to the Keltoi there, when Caesar went. I tried to tell them that it was better to live with the Romans than to die resisting them. I told them that Caesar would build them roads, and that Gallic ships would bring our goods and Rome's to their lands. That they could sell their tin and other goods in return. I told them of our war, and how it was futile to fight this Rome. They put me in chains; I was their hostage, not an ambassador to them like I went to them. Yes, I served Caesar there.

"Then while we were there, our neighbors in Gaul rebelled. They killed seven thousand Romans and besieged other garrisons and Caesar went on the war road until he destroyed them. Then he came back to the Belgae and put his armies with us again. I did not serve Caesar then. His general, Labienus summoned me for a meeting. There he tried to assassinate me. Caesar claimed that he knew nothing of this but I know better. I carry the wounds of that attempted murder.

"I am no friend of Rome. I was once and my tribe profited from it. But now, I've seen our Keltoi neighbors slaughtered and our people abused. We do not share in this Roman friendship anymore and now I ride to end the Roman presence in our lands. I go with my Atrebates and all who would go with me. You Nervii are fierce warriors; if you sit and watch this from your land and let us die, the Romans will be back for you someday. You have felt their lash, and you will again.

"I am Commius; I am King of the Atrebates and the Morini. I go to kill all the Romans at Alesia in the land of the Gauls. All who ride with me will kill Romans. I will kill Caesar myself."

PAT MIZELL

DAY 39

Sedullos and the other kings and war chiefs of Gaul were met by the same questions everywhere they went. "If we send all our men to Alesia, who's going to feed them? And who's going to feed us if they're not here to work the farms? A lot of the harvest is in, but not all; we can't send our food and all our men to Alesia." The old men of the councils allowed some men to go, but only the single ones who wanted to go and they weren't warriors, for the most part.

* * * * *

Vercingetorix and Ladia lay in bed late that morning. The two boys came in and jumped in with them and they were all together. It wouldn't last long though, the boys soon got bored and ran outside to play, and Vercin turned to more serious matters.

"Ladia, the druidae are coming for you and the boys. Draius will take care of you." She didn't answer because she knew what was soon to come. "No arguments." He continued.

"When?" she replied.

"In three days."

There was much to talk about and plans to make. It was noon before they left their house. There was sadness all over Alesia that day; many were suffering.

We gathered that afternoon at Bross's house; we, the ones who had started it all. Gerromir, Vercin, and me.

"I want to ask you as my friends, not as your king, to see to my family if I'm not able to. I won't leave Alesia unless I can ride into a free Gaul; maybe you won't either, but if any of us survive we have to take care of those left behind. I'm sending Ladia to the druidae, and Bross, don't you think Mirandia should go with her." Bross responded to that by saying,

"Vercin, would you bring your boys here tomorrow? I have something to give them." Brossix brought out the little swords and Vercin was very pleased. Gerromir left; he had met a woman.

She lived with her daughter in Alesia, but she was of the Helvetii. Her husband and sons had been killed at Bibracte trying to save the family and they had fled to here six years ago. Gerromir's family was dead for the last five. Gerromir went to the tavern where she worked; we all knew her and liked her. When it closed for the afternoon, Gerromir and Darla went for a walk and found a place that overlooked the town and the rivers.

"Gerromir, we've got to get Lucia out of here, she's twelve and pretty and you know what will happen to her if the Romans and Germans take this town. I've been through that and can again, but not her. She's all I've had for six years, Gerromir. Now I have you but..."

"You're both going, Darla; I still have friends in the mountains and I'm taking you there. They may be scoundrels but they'll honor you and your daughter. The only danger she'll have will be of her choice. They smiled at each other. They made plans to leave in two days; then they went to her house and made love.

* * * * *

"All the traps are complete, Caesar. The trenches are full of them and I've had smaller ditches dug at random angles that have stakes in them too. They aren't conspicuous and are covered with debris. We've put in patches of spikes in little pits also, scattered throughout all of the trenches. The men call them lilies, but if a Gaul steps on one he won't be stepping any more."

"Good, Egius, you've done well. Now you have to do it all again." Egius stared at Caesar. What did he mean? Were they leaving? A new town to attack?

"More Gauls are coming, Egius. When, I don't know, but I know that those horsemen of Vercingetorix didn't leave here to dodge a fight. They'll come back with help and I've heard that the traitor Commius is raising an army. After all I've done for him, he's turned against me.

"I want you to duplicate what you've done, just in the other direction. If they come, we have to fight two armies and we need two walls. My men will live between them. We're not leaving Alesia. We'll die here or Gaul will die here, but you build me another wall and I'll win."

* * * * *

Vercin stood on the wall and stared across the plain to the Roman camp. "There are sixty thousand Roman soldiers there, Cass. And some Germans and some Remi. I can see every one of them from here, but I don't see any Aedui or Commius or the men I've asked for. I even wonder if those I sent for help will return. We've lost nine thousand men in our attempts to damage Caesar yet he sits there behind his barricade with his traps, pits, and trenches keeping us from him.

"I want you to go with my family when the druidae come for them. They'll need your protection."

I stared at him. "No, I will not. You know they'll be safe with the men Draius sends. And you're not sending me away." He didn't say anything else; he knew I wouldn't go.

At his house, we sat for our evening meal. Ladia was trying to convince her two new young warriors that their trip would be an adventure, but they sensed something was wrong. They both had their new swords through their belts. She was packing what she could carry and they were sullen. "Boys, after we eat let's make you some scabbards for those fine swords. We've got plenty of deer skins around here and I'm a fine craftsman with an awl and some tendons. I'll show you how to make them." We left Ladia and Vercin to themselves that evening. A sense of gloom was creeping through Alesia.

DAY 38

"I'm not going anywhere, Brossix. You're not much but I'm too old and fat to start looking for another man, so I'll just have to keep you alive." Mirandia was baking bread; all of the women in Alesia were doing that constantly every day. There were sixty thousand men there to feed and Vercingetorix was tightly controlling the grain supply. Each man and each of the town got their half loaf a day. The townsfolk cooked soup from the root vegetables left in the cellars of the town, and a little meat once a day. Then the cows started running out and tempers got stretched. Mirandia continued.

"When we leave here we'll leave together so you just keep making your swords and I'll keep cooking. How about we drink some beer tonight and if you're not too tired, and if your fat old woman is still in the mood, she'll make you glad she's still in your bed here in Alesia."

Brossix kept eating his meal but he grinned as he did. "Well, old woman, I expect I can pull together the energy every now and then. Now I know the real reason you won't leave with Ladia; you'd miss my lovemaking, wouldn't you?" Now it was Mirandia's turn to grin. They had met when he was a young Legionary and she was a tavern girl of the garrison town. That had been long ago.

"Those little boys were so proud of the swords you made them. They were out in the courtyard when I went over this morning, just a swinging and thrusting just like you goats do when you practice. Are they leaving tomorrow?"

"I think Cass is going to take them; Vercin's tried to get him to but Cass doesn't want to leave him. It's a day to where the druidae are and a day back, but nothing's going on here that someone else can't handle. All we're doing is bleeding or sitting."

* * * * *

In the Roman camp, Caesar was watching the placement of his ballistae. They were sighted in at the main trench, but marks

171

were made on the ground where they were to be moved to when the Gauls made it to the next obstacles. Two more ditches, one filled with water, and traps and hidden stakes all in between.

The ballistae were well inside the Roman walls, placed where their missiles and rocks could clear the barricade, and be hidden from the Gauls' sight. There were over two hundred of them, not counting the almost three hundred in the towers. Mounds of rocks were stacked by each and assignments were given for four man crews. Two to draw the winches, and two to load the stone and spears in them. A thousand missiles a minute would go into the Keltic lines while they struggled to get over the trenches.

Every ten feet along the back of the wall facing the Gauls was a scorpio. When the attack started, they'd be carried up to the top and when the ballistae stopped and the Gauls got near, thousands of arrows would be fired into their faces. The ones who made it through that would be met with fifty thousand pila thrown by the twenty five thousand men on the wall.

The warriors who finally made it to the top of their ladders would then be met with Roman steel; wielded by the finest army in the world. The men of Alesia sat in the taverns and drank their beer and stolen Italian wine and argued about who were the most ferocious.

* * * * *

Gerromir and I led a raid on a Roman cavalry camp. They were situated along the rivers and didn't have the usual fortifications of a typical Legion camp. But they had hard men and vicious Germani. It turned into a melee that left many of our horsemen to stay behind when we left; hundreds of Gauls lay on the ground and hundreds of our horses were lost to become Roman mounts. We rode back in the main gate of Alesia, those of us left. A few survivors walked in later.

DAY 37

Gerromir and Darla made their plans. They would leave tomorrow morning early for his mountain hideout. There were men there he trusted. They wouldn't find with us, but they would fight Romans; most of them were escaped slaves from the Transalpine areas and they weren't going back into chains again. Some women were there too, mostly the women of the wild tribes of the mountains and they fought too. Darla and her daughter would be safe there; there might even be some of their kinsmen, the Helvetii, around. The remnants of that tribe were everywhere.

I left Alesia with Ladia and her children. Two young druidae had come for them, but I went along. It would be good to see Draius one last time. The boys wore their swords thrust through their belts. They were so proud to ride like warriors, armed for the fight. It made the leaving easier for Ladia. We went at dawn. A long day's ride was ahead of us to get to the forest where the druidae were. Vercin watched from the wall as we rode away; Ladia didn't look back.

* * * * *

Quintus and Pexius had the day off; soldiers didn't get many in Caesar's army. They went down to the river and after they took off their armor they cut some saplings and dug some grubs and worms from the riverbank.

"They'll beat us if we're caught without our armor, Quintus."

The older man kind of shrugged and said back, "I think Caesar's got more to worry about than us right now."

Pexius was quieter than he usually was; Quintus had worried himself when he was a young legionary. But now, he had accepted that his fate was in the hands of the gods and Caesar. Or maybe a Gaul somewhere in Alesia.

"We'll have enough for a feast tonight, Pex. These fish are hungry today and so am I. They're probably tired of eating Gauls everyday, and these worms are treats for them." The two men laughed; there weren't many things to laugh about these days. Eighty thousand Gauls sat in front of them and a lot more were on the way.

"My general won't let us down, Pexius. The man's a genius and he wouldn't be sitting here if he thought he'd lose. He wants to get home too."

"I know, Quintus, but we've been digging for two weeks now and still we aren't through."

"Every trench we dig and every post we put up will save a life. Everywhere I've been as a soldier, we do it, and those barricades have saved me in all those places. I know everybody, especially the newer men, would rather storm a town than sit in our holes, but in the end it's who's alive, not how you did it. The loot will be there for us either way."

Pexius pulled in a huge fish. It alone would feed the squad, and they sat under a tree and uncorked their canteens. Someone had lifted some uncut wine. The sun and the wine soon did their damage and the two men napped. The two Morini hidden across the river watched from the shadows, but decided it wasn't worth the gamble.

* * * * *

The boys were tired and starting to nod off; the two druidae put them behind them on their mounts and led the boys' horses. My men and I rode with our hands on our swords

"Ladia, I'll take care of him. When Commius and the others get here, we'll destroy Caesar, and this time next year you'll have your own Roman slave to wait on you."

"I don't want a slave, Cass, I want to go back to my farm. I want to see my mother and father. I want my sons to grow up tending our cattle and raising our wheat; and I want Vercingetorix sitting by my fire at night and in my bed. I want you to live with us or go back to druidae if that is your wish. I'm tired of seeing thousands of soldiers squabbling, boasting, and getting drunk every day. I want to see the Arverni walking into the markets with smiles on their faces and taking home fruit and vegetables and leading young ewes full of milk for their children.

"I want to ride into town with my family and gossip with the women at the wells. I want to see my children playing with other children, not riding through the forest with swords in their belts, terrified and missing their father. I'm sick of this. I'm sick of riding a horse and eating someone else's bread and sleeping in someone else's house. I'm sick of seeing my husband becoming an old man before my eyes and people dying all around me."

"It will end soon, Ladia." That was all I could think of to say.

* * * * *

We found Draius and the others that night, just before dark. Ladia never said another word on our journey; it was a long day. The druidae put Vercin's family in a hut and then we talked long into the night. There were a lot druidae there; in our special place in the forest.

DAY 36

The druidae lived among the others of their tribes, but we had private places in the forests. Much has been told about our roles, but we were mostly the judges and advisors to the kings and chiefs of our societies. We spoke with each other and with our gods and tried to determine a path for our people to take. Now, with our land in turmoil, most of the druidae had come here, to the place where we met to discuss events without others around; those who didn't know or understand the things we did.

A druida was selected as a child, as I've said, for various reasons. A few had shown an ability to understand things that others couldn't, or even see things that were yet to come. I was from a family of kings, but wouldn't be one as long as Vercingetorix lived. Draius said I showed other gifts as a young child, but I was too young to understand that when I first came.

A druida novitiate spent many, many, years studying the past. We Kelts could read and write in the language of the Greeks but discouraged the use of such by others. It had long been our belief that people who wrote of things often confused the true events; while we learned our history and that of others through our own memories; and only from another druida.

A druidae was expected to use the events of the past and the knowledge of present matters to understand the world we lived in better; and often what might transpire in the future. Some, like Draius, knew and saw what was to come. He was special, as were the few that attained that level. It never came to most, but if that ability existed in a young man, it took many years to develop himself and his gift. He always told me I would have that gift some day.

As boys, we learned from songs and poems; remembering was easier that way. In our normal lives we didn't war, or farm, or do any of the things that most of our men did. We could travel to other places and learn from them; we met and talked and all of us knew what one did. We had places all over Gaul in

177

which we met, and once a year, our chief druida would go to Britannia and Hispaniola to discuss events with our own.

* * * * *

Ladia was welcomed. The druidae wives were there, and some children, so the glen was comfortable for her and her children. There were always a few huts and shelters in Druidaea but more had been added during the present wars. Caesar didn't want the druidae influencing the folk, so we went to the forests. Our gods were there with us in the trees.

I spent the day discussing things with Draius and the other senior druidae; the feeling was not as light as it had been in Alesia. Draius felt we had to prepare ourselves for all things. He had been to Rome and other cities outside our lands. He had even been to the Greeks' world and beyond. I was a warrior now; I just listened unless he asked me of the matters of Alesia. I told him the way they were; as I saw them.

"We've tried to make the Romans leave, Draius, but they won't. Caesar sits outside our fortress and acts like he's going to be there forever. The Roman ships and barges come up our rivers, full of food and the other things the Legions need. We stop them, but more come. Rome uses the roads and bridges that they said they were building in our friendship to bring in the materials of war and take out our riches and our people, in chains, as slaves. We'll have to kill them all. Vercin thinks this."

"You can't kill them all, Vercassive. Challenging the Roman Empire is an affront to their people. I think some of their Senate are anxious to bring Caesar back; but some of them, and most of the common Romans are dazzled by the glory of conquest; and the riches that conquerors bring back to Rome. Their society has gotten used to living off the wealth of other people. They were farmers once, and merchants, but now exist by taking from others. That, and making us their slaves.

"The only way we can win is to make it too expensive for the masters of Rome. When war costs them more than they receive, they'll leave. The lives of their armies mean nothing to them. All of Italy and the conquered lands want to be Roman soldiers; they dream of the wealth of the plunder. I worry about this present situation. Do you think we can win at Alesia?"

178

DAY 35

I had a long ride back to think of that question. I had no one to talk to that day; my men were loyal to me but I was supposed to be a leader; not one who showed fear or uncertainty so I couldn't share my concerns with them. Alesia was still there at the end of our journey, and so was Caesar.

Every day the ballistae and scorpio were fired a few times to test for accuracy. The weakness of artillery was in the drawstring that was the heart of its power and trueness. The rest of the weapon was wood, fastened together with iron nails and bands, but the drawstring that propelled the missile was made out of sinew or twisted material that made a cord. Dampness affected it, even just the natural nighttime fog or morning mist. Extreme care was taken to keep them dry but since they had to be ready to shoot on a few moments notice, they were always subject to the weather.

There were specalists in charge of each machine and each morning a rock or two or an arrow would be shot at the specified target predetermined by the placement of the piece. If the missile fell short, the string was replaced and retested. When the placement and equipment were correct, then the larger ballistae were locked into place. Most were aimed at the large trench but would be taken backward to another predetermined spot as the enemy neared. All of this was intended to kill attackers but the demoralizing effect of having a hailstorm of missiles falling around were just as effective as the object itself. It caused men to turn and run or hide behind something while their fellow attackers were killed. Either way, they break the charge.

"We stand here and watch them practice, Cass, but we can't practice crossing those trenches or running across that field. Somehow we just have to do it when the time comes."

I don't know how men can charge a wall. Riding a horse with a sword in your hand is one thing; we all grew up doing that. You had a rage up and the horse between your legs gave you a sense of power, and you could always turn and ride the other way. But running across a field with the rocks and arrows coming at you head on, knowing there was a man waiting to kill you is another matter. I guessed I would soon learn. We'd have to cross those ditches, carry ladders, climb up, and then face death.

* * * * *

The little village sat in the lands where the Helvetii had once lived, close to the lands of Germani. When the Helvetii left, they had burned their houses and fields so no one could have the benefit of them, but the Germans didn't care. They just needed land and could rebuild houses. Not many Helvetii came back, most of the two hundred and fifty thousand that Caesar had stalked were dead, and the Germans had trickled in, family by family and clan by clan.

They built their huts close to each other, and improved them as time went by. They walked to their fields every day and back in the evening. After their meal, if the sun was still up and the weather nice, they would come out of their houses to walk together and gossip at the well. Most were there when the Gauls struck them.

The Boii had been watching them all afternoon, from the nearby forest. At dusk, when the villagers were milling about in conversations and relaxation the Boii drew their swords and started their horses at a trot across the field of barley. Then into their gallop and they were on top of the Germans before they could even run for their hoes and rakes. All of the Germans were slaughtered and left where they lay. There wasn't much loot in the village, mainly just some food. The Gauls left the rest; it was of no interest to them. That wasn't why they had come. They had come to kill. They didn't even bother to burn the houses.

DAY 34

The Roman Senate left their assembly walking in small groups through the Forum acknowledging the greetings and smiles of the people on their way to their daily business. It was a beautiful September day in Rome and Cato invited two of the men to go home with him for refreshment. Cato was a wealthy man, but you wouldn't know it. He lived very frugally and some called him the only honest man in Rome. It was quite a walk to his house but there were things that needed discussing.

"I heard that a courier arrived today, Pompey didn't tell us of the news. I suppose he'll speak to the Senate tomorrow, but this is what you'll hear. Caesar was defeated in an attack on a Gaul stronghold and is retreating with all of his legions. At least now his insatiable appetite for power is checked; for this year anyway." Cato took a sip of his cheap wine and a bite of his bread. It was warm with cheese and herbs on it, just the way he liked.

"Caesar has a lot of friends, Cato, and the people adore him. It's too bad that he's turned on his own; we've made him rich." The old Senator remarked.

"I care not a whit for who gets rich; it's The Republic that concerns me, and our constitution is the heart of that." Cato went on. "Caesar has no respect for the hundreds of years of history that have gone into making us what we are now. There are things that need to be done, but not by a dictator or king; as it seems he wants to be."

The next day, the Senate met at their usual time; another courier had ridden in during the night and the Counsel Pompey, felt vindicated now by his reluctance the day before to give an early report. Pompey spoke. "Caesar found Labienus and they're now laying siege to the Gauls at a place called Alesia. He says he is hopelessly outnumbered but still seems very optimistic. He thinks the Gauls will disintegrate in a month or two; they aren't known for their patience anyway and they seemingly have a long time planning anything of more than an immediate nature.

Scipio rose. "Cato, what is your opinion? Should we start planning Caesar's victory parade or his funeral?" Most of the senators laughed at the remark, but a few were strangely silent in a place not known for silence.

* * * * *

Over the years, Draius and the other druidae had explained to me and all the other novitiates the history of Rome. The druidae had explained how that empire differed now from what it had once been. I had a lot of time to think of that while I stood on the walls of Alesia and watched Caesar's army work.

"Rome became a place when thirty five tribes united, Vercassivellaunus; in a way completely opposite from how our tribes lived. They united and drove the Etruscans away, they drove the Greeks away, then they drove our Gauls away, or made them their subjects. And when the last threat came from Carthage, they trembled for awhile, but destroyed it in the end. They were tribes of farmers, not warriors, but would unite and form an army to defend themselves against others. Our tribes argue among ourselves for leadership and dominance while their tribes fought as one. That's why they won.

"Those thirty five tribes still rule Rome; they're called 'Senators' now and they don't farm anymore, they just rule others. And they don't get their hands dirty and bloody in war, they hire others to do it. It used to be that their farmers would lay down their hoes and grab a spear or a sword and go to war for the good of all, then return and pick them up and make their living. Rome grew; some of those farmers came home with slaves to do the work for them.

"As Rome grew they felt a need for things that they couldn't have individually, like roads and viaducts and ships to trade with other lands, so taxes were levied on all. Then the day came when the farmers who lived by their own labor returned home and their fields were in disarray or their crops had failed. They still had taxes to pay and they had to eat. So the farmers who had prospered bought those lands and made those people a class different from themselves.

"They were all still Romans, and all still part of those thirty five tribes, but some were beholden to others and some owed

182

money. Most looked to the prosperous ones to tell them what to do and how to choose their leaders and while Rome's citizens were still free to choose their leaders it, by the natural course of events, Rome became a place where the elite and wealthy ruled."

DAY 33

I stood on that wall and watched those thirty-five tribes build their fortifications. I wondered how many of those sixty thousand men even knew who ran Rome. Rome was the largest city in the world and most of these hard men had never even been there, much less been born in it. Draius kept in contact with the Keltoi who lived and thereabouts; he and the other wise men of the druidae understood better than even most Romans how that empire worked. I had thought about it a lot on my long, lonely, journey back to Alesia.

I had seen the Roman legions for two years now. I had seen how that ruthless efficient machine worked, and my people couldn't match that. All we could do was to try out killing them. Here, at Alesia, we would decide things. Either we killed them all or they went home. Or they killed us.

* * * * *

The barge came up the river, slaves poling it along and steersmen keeping it away from the banks. It was full of grain from Africa and other goods that the legions needed. Gerromir watched it move along; he knew where the depots and ports were; he had loaded more of these boats than most.

"When they get to that sharp turn up ahead, the current will push them close to the shore. We'll be there. Throw your spears at the ones in uniform, try not to kill the slaves, but don't let that rule your attacks. If the ones not in uniform resist, kill them, if they run, let them go. But kill everything wearing red"

Gerromir didn't know of the Roman escorts on either side of the river. The Roman navy had started sending small patrols on horseback with each boat. Most of those men were the Remi who had remained loyal to Caesar, but there were others with them who worked for gold. The more Keltic heads they brought back, the more gold they earned.

The Remi chief who led the horsemen on the same side of the river on which Gerromir was situated saw the Gauls moving onto the river back, long before the barge arrived. He didn't attack them then; he didn't care if the barge was taken or not. He and his renegades were there for the loot and the heads of the Gauls. He silently gathered his group high up on the hill above the ambush site; at a place where the Gauls raiding party would pass by after their attack.

Gerromir and his warriors attacked the barge. It was a complete surprise. The barge had come around the bend in the little river. It was only five or so feet from Gerromir's ambush site in the reeds. His spears hit nearly every one of the eight Romans on board. The boatmen jumped into the water; they wanted no part of this. Then the Gauls grabbed the barge and finished off those left alive. They used their swords, or twisted and pushed the spears sticking out of the Romans. Gerromir cut the ropes of the remaining slaves and told them to take what food they could carry and go to the mountains. He stopped at that. "We don't want any more mouths to feed, you get out of here. It's not your war. I'm taking all the armor and weapons with me; just grab some grain and bacon, and go. There are men there who will help you; just don't be carrying any weapons or that greeting will be short."

The slaves helped the Gauls throw the sacks of grain into the river. The raiding party couldn't take it back to Alesia, as bad as it was needed their. They had to keep raiding. They took what they could carry for themselves, and so did the slaves, but none was left for the next Roman boat to find. Then Gerromir set fire to the barge, the slaves left, and the Gauls rode into the ambush.

* * * * *

We had all our men making wooden spears and ladders; most had swords. When we attacked, we would fill the tops of that Roman barricade with our spears and whatever else we could throw at them, but anything we had with us, had to be carried across those ditches and over that four hundred feet of dead man's land. Brossix showed the tribesmen how to harden the wooden stakes in the fire after they were sharpened; they would do. We had to have ladders to get on top of that wall, and we'd have to carry them too. We would have to attack. Caesar was barricaded there in his new fort and we saw no help for us arriving. We were just sitting around with our stomachs

186

grumbling and our warriors well past the grumbling stage. It was odd; we didn't have enough to eat but the taverns never ran out of beer. Hungry armed men and beer made an unhealthy mixture.

DAY 32

"There's a gold chest there in Caesar's tent and I'm going to have some of it." Ambix was a Mediomatrici chief who had brought two thousand men to Alesia. He and his clansmen sat around their fire and ate their bowls of porridge. "This is dogshit; I want the fresh bread of my woman and the vegetables from my cellar. This time of year the boar and deer are fat, but we sit here eating mush. But we'll find riches in there; Caesar carries his fortune with him, so go far his tent when we get in. Soon, my brothers, we'll be home and spending Roman gold. And they have slaves that will be ours too; they're the same as gold, those Greeks and Thracians."

* * * * *

Two of those slaves were busy that day. One, named Spanius was supervising the unloading of the supply wagons. He had been a merchant in Hispania who ran caravans in and out of the mountain valleys where the olives and grapes were grown. Nine years ago, his tribe had rebelled against Rome and a caravan he was leading was massacred by Caesar's cavalry; he was taken as a slave, probably because he was older and didn't fight. He was always beside the Roman officer who was in charge of supplies and told him what orders he should give.

The other was a Greek who kept Caesar's correspondence and official documents moving to Rome and back. Three other scribes worked with him. All of them were educated in the languages of the Greeks and Romans and their chief allies in other places. The two men were friends and ate together at noon if their duties allowed.

"How goes the reporting today, Xirtes?"

"The usual," replied the Greek. "Caesar dictating glorified accounts of his triumphs and battles for the Senate's consumption. I don't know if they believe it all but Caesars makes sure that his couriers know what they're taking and it doesn't take long for them to spread Caesar's version of events

189

in the taverns and gatherings along the way. Caesar's the people's god now, he and Pompey."

Spanius understood that. He had gone with Caesar to Rome last winter to give requisitions to the merchants there. Rome's government only ruled the conquered territories. No one actually did anything. The rich men who had the concessions made all the decisions. All of the commercial activity and equipping the army was given to the rich men who had bribed the proper senators; even the taxes from the empire were privately collected in return for a fee paid to the powers in charge.

"I don't know how they think they can rule the world forever when none of them grow up knowing anything about war or how to farm or do anything but sit and collect money."

"They hire people to do it for them, Spanius, and make men like us their slaves. There are no Roman farmers anymore, just the ex soldiers and slaves. They pay the men who lead the tribes of Rome for the privilege of digging in their own soil. But, they have conquered our worlds and continue to look for more. There's Persia left, and the green isles, and then some day they'll have to fight the Germani for what's left. But I write Caesar's letters and write down his words and you tell his officers how to move their goods and we eat better than most and are still alive. I never thought I would be after that raid on my town in Syracuse that day."

"Would you pass me that fruit?"

* * * * *

Gerromir had just cut off the right thumb of the man he took back to his hidden camp outside Alesia. "How many groups like yours and how many Roman patrols on the river?" The man started babbling like an idiot; he didn't care what happened to them, he just wanted to live. But he didn't.

Gerromir's hard men weren't expecting the ambush, but it didn't take them long to react and the renegades were cut down man by man; all but one. Now he was dead at Gerromir's feet. Gerromir had his own way of sneaking into Alesia and he went to Vercingetorix with this news. "Try to find Sedullos and get some of his men. Sweep the rivers, and try to bring back any

190

food you find. Make the slaves and the Romans you capture carry it; maybe we can bribe the Remi into letting us bring some in here."

* * * * *

Gerromir readied Darla for their escape. Alesia was completely surrounded by Romans and the Remi horse but the druidae that came for Ladia had kinsmen with the Remi; who as a favor to the gods, and some of the druidae gold, would turn their heads for small groups sneaking in and out; as long as the Romans couldn't see them. "Be ready to go at dawn; it's a long ride to meet my tribesmen and I have to be back by night. Take some clothes, and nothing else. Those men who live in the mountains have all that is necessary to live; and they know ways to get more. Take couple of blankets though; I'll have food for us." Gerromir was going to miss Darla, and her daughter Lucia. But he wouldn't have another family of his killed, or try to survive alone if he was. She'd be safe with those men and if he didn't come for her one of them would take her for his woman; at least the girl wouldn't be raped unless she wanted to be.

* * * * *

Spanius completed the unloading of the wagons, and although he hadn't done any of the heavy work, he was covered with dust and grime. Xirtes would meet him later, after the officers had their baths; then they could wash their own day away. That was the only time the slave had to himself, when his master was asleep. At least they lived more comfortably than the poor people who weren't attached to an officer of high rank. They had nothing to call their own. Only their lives, which weren't much anymore. When they went to the bath tent later, after the evening horns blew, they luxuriated in the water that the Roman generals had used a few hours before; and ate the remains of their meals. It was still better than most had that day.

191

DAY 31

The ladders had to be thirty feet long if they were to reach the top of the Roman barricade. That meant a lot of timber had to be cut and shaped. The ladders had to be strong enough to hold a man on every rung but as light as possible because men would have to carry them for hundreds of feet under artillery fire from the ballistae in the Roman camp. The trees inside the walls of Alesia had all been cut down; timbers in houses were stripped out, and every saw and axe in the town was in use.

When we attacked, all the men in Alesia would pour out the gates carrying ladders, bundles of sticks to throw in the trenches, and their weapons. Every ditch or other obstacle we met would create a massing of men. We had to get across as quickly as we could, but we couldn't fill trenches ten miles long or carry a ladder for every man. These things had to be planned. We tried to solve this the way we always did, by making each tribe responsible for their sector of ground.

* * * * *

Gerromir and five of his warriors sat on their horses outside Darla's house. He finally got down and went inside to get the two women. "What's in this bag, Darla, it's heavier than clothes should be."

"Just some things that I want to keep, Gerromir." Lucia was ready; it was a big adventure for her and finally the three went outside.

"I'm not a very good rider, said Darla.

"You don't have to be very good, just stay on top of the damn thing until we reach Gutuater's men. Then you walk all you want because I'll be bringing your horses back here. You can't ride them into those mountains anyway. My friends there will be walking."

They rode all morning and stopped to eat. The five warriors sat with their backs to women and watched the skyline while they had their bread; there was a little cheese too. "My rear hurts," whined Lucia.

"I know it hurts, girl, but you've been a Helvetii warrior today and it's not far now. Gutuater will be close, but he's being careful. When I hand you and your mother off to him, you'll have to obey him. There are ways you have to live in the mountains that you're not used to, so just listen to him. It'll be hard for you there, but it won't be for long. This business with Caesar will be settled within a few weeks."

Renius and Corpitus sat and looked over the valley below. The other two men were scouring the tree lines on the ridges around it. Satisfied, they came down off the mountain and started walking. They saw the mounted men coming after two miles, and they were flying the blue banner that Gerromir had told Gutuater they would have. The renegades sat down and waited, and when the group rode up they rose and greeted them; as brothers and sisters.

Gerromir spoke to the four men. "You have responsibility for my family, and they are my family. I'll be back for them in a few weeks or a month or so and there better not be a hair on their heads out of place when I do. They'll carry their own weight but remember they're city folk so be patient; they know to do what you tell them when you're on that mountain. Just be careful of what you tell them to do because I'll be back.

After a brief rest the two groups parted; Gerromir and his men leading two spare horses and the women and Renius's men walking back to their hideaways in the mountains.

The Remi in the trees watched. Their horses were tied on the other side of the ridge line and Squavi and his men were well hidden; they had taken off their armor so there would be no reflections from the sun. They had come to this spot two days before; on a five day observation patrol. They had no supplies other than the bread and bacon they carried, with their allowances of wine and some cheese and onions. They were not here to fight, but to watch, and after their five days to return to their camp at Alesia and report on the comings and goings of the Gauls.

The Remi leader sat with his second in command and watched; there were four men walking back to the mountain, but they were lightly armed and wore no armor. The two women were of no matter in a fight. They had seen the walkers when they emerged from the mountain and then watched the mounted men ride to greet them. They had no idea what was going on, but that was not their job; only to observe and report, and to come back to Alesia early if anything of consequence happened. This was not one of those things. Just five mounted men and two women meeting four men walking off the mountain. Nothing of consequence.

Gerromir made it back to Alesia by dark; without the women his warriors could ride fast and hard. Renius's journey was shorter and would have been easy, but just before they reached the rocks two hours later, the Remi patrol appeared out of the trees and massacred them. All but two of them; the women lasted until the morning.

DAY 30

"See that old man there? The one with the red hair? He has been standing at that place on the wall for two days now. He'll leave sometimes and then come back with one or two others, then they'll leave again. But the old man keeps coming back to the same spot." Varimus was the senior officer of the artillery. He had called a meeting of his officers. They were atop one of the towers that faced Alesia.

"He's planning his attack. He's looking at the sector he will advance in. That's why he's there all the time. Look for others on the wall that seem to always be in the same place. The Gauls are planning their attack and the war chiefs are planning their advances. All we have to do is look where they're looking and we'll know where they plan on crossing the trenches. I don't know how many of those crossings they'll have but it won't be sixty thousand of them; just where they're looking." Varimus reported this to Caesar and his men watched the walls of Alesia.

* * * * *

Sedullos had been busy since leaving Alesia. The elders of the tribes might squabble but his men were warriors and they wanted to return to Alesia. They just couldn't get in. Instead, his men attacked every Roman foraging party that left the camp. Then Caesar caught on and started sending the Germans with them.

In their own camp near the Legions' barricade, the Germani were restless. "Are we going to spend all our time chasing Gauls, Urdus? Or are we going to get rich?" The German man had been with Urdus since he went to the Romans but reflected all of their attitudes. They hadn't come to fight for Caesar, but to raid and take. Caesar had given Urdus gold for his services, but little had trickled down to his men; and they were restless.

"Trust Caesar, Hardus, he's promised us riches. When we take that town, all of Gaul will be at our feet and when we strip the lands and kill the Gauls, we'll bring our families back here. All the tribes will join us, but we'll have our pick. You and I will sit as fat old men and watch our Keltoi slaves doing the work in the fields while we sit drinking beer and cracking walnuts."

* * * * *

At Caesar's morning staff meeting, all of the plans and their status were reviewed. "Egius, your report please?"

"The defense works are basically complete, Caesar. Our main trench is twenty feet deep and twenty feet wide with squared walls. There is the slight lip on our side that you requested. The other two trenches are not as big, but with the traps and stakes hidden around and between them, they will suffice. The artillery is sighted in at those three ranges and can be moved or rotated to the field of action.

"The outer ballistae are placed so as to fire down the Gauls line when it reaches the inner ditch. That way, as they make their way across they'll be catching missiles from their left and right while the scorpio come at them head on. Thousands of arrows and rocks will hit them every minute. When the Gauls try to scatter and space themselves the artillery will launch the baskets of stones and lead bullets at them, and fill their areas with hundreds of them at once.

"The inner trench is filled with water diverted from the rivers. We have man-killing stakes at the bottom, and all around there sat in different angles. Now that we know where the Gauls will concentrate their crossings, I have men out at night reinforcing those areas with more of our traps. All in all, it's a killing field. The engines will thin them down and some of them will turn and run and more will be disheartened."

Labienus spoke up. "There will be a lot that aren't. Those men are warriors and don't care about death. They believe they'll come back to life in another body after they die, so we'll have plenty on our hands when they hit our wall."

"That's where you and I come in, Labienus, that's where we kill them." Caesar finished. "Are we protected on all sides now?"

"Yes, General, and I'm bringing the cavalry in. No one will leave and no one will come in; we have the food and forage we need and the men are anxious. They'll take out on the Gauls the weeks of digging and carrying they've endured."

"Good," said Caesar, "Just be sure and let them know who caused their misery; it wasn't me." The men laughed as they left the tent, and then Brutus went to talk to the Germans.

* * * * *

Gobanitio finished his inventory of the stores left in Alesia. The dead and the horsemen who had left earlier had reduced the mouths to feed. But nothing had come in either. Roman and German patrols were everywhere now, and Alesia was sealed in on all sides. There weren't many horses inside now, so that was not a problem. There was no hay left and little millet anyway.

With the work assigned to them mostly done, the Mandubii inside Alesia went back to their complaining; they weren't used to living on soldiers' rations; neither were the soldiers.

DAY 29

Quintus and his seven tent mates were hard, harder than they had ever been, even when they were on the march. Three weeks of labor, twelve hours a day under the September sun of Gaul had toughened them up while at the same time put them in the foul mood that only a battle would cure. They sat that afternoon in various stages of lassitude around their cooking fire. Pieces of a cow were roasting on it; the livestock and cavalry had been brought inside the camp, and some had to be gotten rid of said their officers, to the delight of the men. Fresh baked bread, meat, wine, and beer were good after the day of hard drills.

They had spent the morning in sword drills, the basics they all knew, but Caesar's legions never quit practicing and drilling. That's why they won.

"What will you do on your leave this winter, Pexius?" The new man, Cellus, had never garrisoned before.

"Oh, I'll see my wife and then decide whether I want her to join us in Narbo or whether I want a new one this year." They all chuckled, Pexius was known for never keeping a woman long.

"How much do you think we have in the baggage train? Are we rich yet?"

Quintus snorted at Cellus's remark.

"Come on Quintus, I just want to know. I want to send some money home to my family and I want to have some fun myself."

"You'll have enough, Cellus," said the oldest man, Faris. "This is my fourteenth campaign and it's been the most prosperous year yet. I've got a nice little nest egg waiting for me and this year's plunder will cap it off."

"Are you rejoining, Faris?"

"No, I'm through. And after we finish off the Gauls I don't know where we'd go next."

"Maybe we'll just sit in Rome all winter and wait for Caesar's Triumph." Pexius's entire ambition was to go to Rome. "I hear there's a whorehouse on every block and taverns in between each," he added. Now that would be a winter for me!"

They all knew they had to live through this first. All these men had fought, some for a long time. These men of Gaul were different from the outlaws of Hispania and the wild tribes of the alpines. This fight would open the doors of Alesia to them, and all the riches that lay inside.

* * * * *

"How many fighting men are left?" Vercingetorix had all of the war chiefs in his large inner room. There were over thirty men there, counting Brossix, Gerromir, and me. "How many other mouths do we have?" The men argued and squabbled but Gobanitio was writing. Just before the first fight broke out, Vercin spoke up.

"Gobanitio, what's the situation?" My father rose and addressed us all. All of the men there were similar in some ways; some were young and angry and some were old and scarred from battle, often with each other over the years, but none of them was used to hunger. None was used to being confined within walls, and none had ever attacked a Roman fortification before.

"When we came in here, there were eighty thousand of us, and about twenty thousand townspeople. Between the horsemen who left and those killed we have about fifty thousand now; but the same twenty thousand Mandubii. We have enough food, if we ration it carefully to feed this seventy thousand about a week, maybe a little more. The townspeople have stores hidden away I'm sure, and the men, I expect, know this.

"My storehouses are all I can be sure of; the cattle are gone, the swine are gone; we have some salted meat left and a couple of dozen barrels of turnips and onions, and some beets. But the grain is what I count. We'll be down to the barley soon; the wheat and the millet will be gone in a few days."

I asked, but knew the answer. "Is there any chance of us getting any supplies in?"

Vercin gave me my answer, I think for all to hear, "No, but there's a way we can get some of the mouths and bellies out of here; that's just as good." All of the men roared at that. They wanted to attack now and thought this was their signal. But it wasn't.

DAY 28

Vercin and I went for a ride that morning. There were still areas in the city in which we could ride; not many, but he wanted to talk with me without others bothering him. We hadn't had much of a chance these last few months and soon it could all be ending. We found a little hilltop and we dismounted. We had men watching over us, so we weren't worried; and the Germani were being strangely silent.

"We will have a hard day tomorrow, Cass." I wasn't sure of his meaning but he had been very quiet since the assembly yesterday. "I'm cutting the rations in half, and I'm ordering a search of the Mandubii houses. And no more grain is going to make beer; so the men better drink up what they've got and enjoy it, it's the last they'll see until we either take Caesar's camp or we're in our next life."

"Do you think we'll meet there, Vercin?"

"Caesar's camp or the next life?" He answered and we both laughed; only the gods knew.

We talked of our childhood and our lives, and of our mothers and fathers and of Ladia and the boys. "You have to look after them, Cass. Caesar is not going to let me live but you have to promise me that if it comes to it, you'll find a way to escape. If you love me, you'll do that." I couldn't say much, but I didn't intend to obey him.

* * * * *

"Father, have you heard from Mother?" Gobanitio looked at me; it had been a long time since we had talked as father and son.

"Yes, she's at the farm. I told her to go to the cellar in the woods at the first sighting of any riders" Like a lot of farmers, we always kept a cellar in the woods far from our houses. We used them to store our vegetables for the winter but they were also a refuge for our women. Ours was cleverly disguised and had a cover that looked like the forest floor. Two people could live in there for weeks if they had to; there was food and we put water inside on occasion. If anyone had to hide there, they could get out at night for the necessary things and to see what was happening in the world. Mother was strong; she'd make it. Father should leave and go to her and I told him so; his work here would soon be over. When there wasn't any food left to count, he wouldn't be needed and he was too old to fight anymore.

* * * * *

"Turn that ballista three notches to the right. I want it hitting that spot where the little dip comes out of the trench. They'll be coming up it." The officer had orders for himself and his main assistants to visit every engine every day. He always started with the tower on the left and rode down the line, adjusting the elevation and direction; he had found a damp drawstring one morning and had the four men attached to it beaten; in the middle of the main camp for all to see. The horn signal for summary assembly had been blown and all the men not on watch were there. Rarely was anything overlooked again after the soldiers had seen their own beaten half to death. Lives were at stake.

* * * * *

The Roman camp was settled in for the night. The Roman squad was gambling. Dice were thrown and wine rations were won and lost and the new man Cellus mostly won. A day of luck for him. The horses and the mules were roaming between the barricades and the stink was awful; but they had full bellies and some free time on their hands. Alesia was quiet. Caesar walked the lines; he often did, and the men always greeted him. He knew some of their names and he would hail them back. His generals didn't walk with him; he wanted the men to know that he was the only one that mattered.

DAY 27

The elders of the Mandubii tribe arrived at mid morning. Vercin had sent for them early, he and I were there waiting when they arrived. Gobanitio arrived behind them and all were seated; quickly Vercin spoke.

"This isn't easy so excuse the lack of pleasantries. There aren't any anyway, I don't think. We don't have much food left. I think you know that. No more is coming. Gobanitio has the count but my decision comes down to this. I'm cutting the rations for you. All of you who aren't fighting will get half of the tribesmen. And before you leave here today my men will search your houses for your hidden stores; I know you have food somewhere. As we are here my men are moving about and they'll take everything they find and ration back your share."

"What do you mean, 'our share'?" The old man screamed. "That's our food and this is our town, and you tell us what we can have or not have?"

"Yes, because like it or not, this is your war too. My men are dying every day fighting Romans and I have to try to keep the rest alive. Gobanitio will go over the count with you now. I'm going to see my men. You stay here, there's bread for your noon meal and I'll be back afterwards to make plans with you for this. It's hard, but that's the way I see it."

Vercin and I went to the well; Gerromir and the others already had their orders and were now beginning their searches, and Vercin didn't want to be there while the arguing and yelling started. We sat under the tree and had our own loaf with a bit of bacon. When we saw Gobanitio leaving, we waited a while and then went back. Vercin had guards around the house of course; none of the old men would leave until the searches were complete. I guess the men considered themselves hostages; maybe they were.

When we went inside, they were ready for us. It was obvious that they had a plan when they came in here this morning. Their leader Vegius spoke. "We are leaving here Vercingetorix; you have our town now, we didn't invite you here, but we leave it to you. My people have no part in this war; it's you and the war chiefs of the other tribes that have brought it to all of us. We had no say; you have taken over our lands and tried to make it one land under your rule. We can't stop you, but we can leave." Vercin looked hard at him, but it was all an act, his heart was breaking.

"Then leave in the morning, but you take nothing with you. One loaf of bread a person only; Caesar will let you through his lines and you can reach your kin. You may leave now and may the gods accompany you; your town will be here for you when this is over."

They left. They knew when they came in what they would do and I think Vercin did also. Things had gone too smoothly. Maybe we could survive now; the townspeople would anyway, we had to hope Commius came. Vercin and I walked to Brossix's shed.

DAY 26

Caesar was summoned at dawn. The gates of Alesia had been opened and people were streaming slowly but steadily out of them. Labienus looked at Caesar when he arrived on the wall. "It's mostly women and children, Caesar, some men but none in armor and no weapons that I see."

The Romans watched the people of Alesia walk down their hill and cross their wall and ditch; they started assembling at the great trench of the Roman defense. "Go down there Antonious. Brutus, you go with him. Take someone who can speak their language."

When the Roman Equestris led by the generals trotted up, they saw thousands of people sitting on the ground. They had their bags, and they looked serene. It was all over for them now. Marcus Antonius and Decimus Brutus rode out from the column. A group of old men walked forward to meet them and the Roman generals rode up to the trench.

"We speak for Mandubii, my lords, we are leaving this place; it's not our war. We want you to know that."

"Who's leaving and what's your name?" Antonious asked in the Latin that the old man had used.

* * * * *

The Roman column rode back to their fort; Caesar was not at the wall, so they went to his tent. They were admitted quickly by his guards and found him relaxing at a table with a glass of wine. He offered them one and called for his servants to bring them refreshments. Brutus was senior so he made the report. After he finished, the food arrived. Caesar passed around the tidbits of cheese and meat and hot bread with butter melted over it.

"Eat up. You've still got work to do today. I know now that we've won this war. I knew it when Vercingetorix took his men inside those walls, but now I see it. Soon we'll be marching back to Norbo and then Rome, and you two will be riding through the streets of Rome with me; in my Triumph.

209

"Finish, and rest for a while. Then go back and tell those people that they aren't going anywhere; they can go back through their gates, I don't care, but they aren't leaving here now. When they go, if they go, it will be in chains as Roman slaves and I don't have the time or the food for that now."

* * * * *

The Roman cavalrymen were poised on the flanks of the trench. The Third Legion came out the gate and lined the inside of it. The people of Alesia watched them and then a Roman Centurion under the official banner rode with a contingent of men rode to the meeting place. The old men came and the Roman spoke.

"You can go back inside or you can sit here and rot. The artillery of Rome is pointed at you now and if you attempt to cross, you'll die. If you do make it across our men will ride you down. If you make it past them, our Legion will kill you, and if you then manage to escape the Germani will have you. We have no other answer for you." With that, he turned his horse and the column followed him back into the fort of Caesar. The Centurion reported to Antonious who was in the bath tent. Then he went to his evening meal. The Mandubii sat there as darkness approached.

DAY 25

This morning, they were still sitting there. By midday, some had gone back to the walls of Alesia but the gates didn't open for them. By dark, they were crying and screaming to the men on the wall to help them; but they were still there when the lights of Alesia and the Roman camp had been extinguished that night

PAT MIZELL

DAY 24

Marcus Bibulus and his followers sat in his house; Pompey had joined them, as had several other prominent members of the Senate. It began with a sumptuous affair that lasted for hours. His cooks had performed masterfully with all the dishes to which the privileged Romans looked forward.

The guests had arrived in late afternoon and after Bibulus's slaves had washed their feet and hands, they were ushered into the main room where all sat on couches around a magnificent table laden with the preparations for a feast. After some tidbits and flavored wine, the serving slaves began to bring in the courses. There were arrays of oysters and fruits from abroad and mounds of the vegetables that the Romans loved.

When the main courses arrived, they were accompanied by household horns that announced a special event. There were platters of pigeons and ducks and even huge roasts, but the centerpiece was a magnificent peacock, with the once proud feathers arrayed in a replica of its former self.

The dining and drinking lasted for hours. As some dozed, others talked. In the last hour, the business of the affair was finally conducted. Bibulus led the discussion, as was the custom, but Cato was there too; and all the old families of Rome had at least one member in attendance.

"Is there any news from Gaul?"

When no one answered, Pompey finally spoke up. "I had one of my couriers talk to a person who is there and Caesar evidently thinks he has things under control. He's outnumbered, he says, but you know Caesar and his exaggerations. He's trying to starve the Gauls so they have to come out and attack him. If they do, he'll win. No matter how many of them there are, a concentrated army of Roman Legions is going to win."

"How many effective fighting men does he have? I know he's got ten legions but they've been in the field all year in battle after battle and they have to be decimated?" The senator who asked that question had never really been in battle, but liked for people to think he knew what was important in one. "It's not the numbers, Jalus, it's the concentration of power and the discipline that evokes that. And even my legions couldn't overwhelm those of Caesar's; he's a good general," Pompey interjected.

Cato asked, "What will Caesar want if he conquers Gaul?"

Galba answered, "Just Rome, then eventually the rest of the world." All the men laughed at that, but Pompey's laughter was very mild, and Cato's less than that.

* * * * *

The Mandubii were starting to die. It was three days now in the hot September sun without anything given to them but the water from the trench. When one woman tried to crawl out the other side, a ballista fired a large rock that landed within several feet of her. Dozens of people were already dead, mostly the old ones, and a few children. The wailing and crying were only relieved by the screams of the women who had lost their young.

DAY 23

The Roman slave trader approached Caesar's tent and asked to see him. The legionary asked his name and business then went inside and returned to announce permission. Caesar was dictating to his scribes; two were busy writing.

"Yes, Sates, what?"

"General," said the man, "I beg your pardon for intruding, but I just want to point out that a fortune in slaves is dying out there. Could I possibly have your permission to at least take the prime ones?"

"Don't be impatient, Sates, there'll be enough for you soon enough. Most of them aren't fit for Rome anyway, just old ones and children, and the women too ugly for Vercingetorix's men to want to keep. And I don't have the time to haggle with you over the prices right now anyway, much less try to figure out how to feed and guard them. Let them go, there'll be plenty for you when I'm done. By the way, "What is the going rate now for a male slave right now? One to work in the fields? Say about thirty or forty thousand of them? Can the market support that number all at once?"

* * * * *

The men in Alesia were all drunk. Vercingetorix had released the last of the beer and ale; it was the only thing keeping them from going insane from the screams outside the gates. "We have nothing to give them Cass," he said to me, "they made their choice, and it was Caesar. He rejected them and now only the gods can determine their fates."

* * * * *

Commius rode with eleven thousand men. He had promised Vercingetorix to bring two hundred and fifty thousand. A lot of the Belgae kings said their tribes would come right behind him and the Aedui would be there at Bibracte waiting for him and maybe some others along the way. He was furious at some of his neighbors but each tribe decided their own matters, and some pointed out that the Gauls hadn't come to help them six years before.

The horsemen rode the roads that had carried the essence of Gaul to Rome and they crossed the bridges built over the rivers to do the same. Each mile and each day built a fury in Commius and his men that made up for the number that weren't coming. They would be enough. Besides, he Aedui would be there.

And they were; over thirty thousand of them, them and their subject tribes. They were ready for a fight too; and when Commius rode through the city on his way to Alesia, he at last had an army with him.

* * * * *

Gutuater and the other renegades came out from the rocks at the base of the mountain. They had seen the bodies below and were being very cautious. Renius and his Venetti had been gone too long; he knew what he would find. They scoured the tree line for two hours looking for any movement or reflection. They had seen none, but Renius probably hadn't either.

There were six bodies; mostly eaten by the wolves and birds.

"Those two must be the women they came to meet, but my count says Gerromir wasn't with them; either that or he's taken."

"No one would take him again, Gutuater, He wasn't here." The other man was following the hoof prints that led away from the site; "It wasn't Romans, must have been some of there tribesmen who happened on them. The trail comes and goes back to that group of trees up on that hill."

DAY 22

They had been drilling hard all day: the basics; sword thrusts, the shield wall, how to protect a position and shove the man ahead into the enemy ranks. The men of Caesar's ten legions went to their tents for food and rest, now that their day was over. Over for all but the guards and riders.

Quintus Cicero hurried through his bath; Labienus had invited him and a few others to his tent for refreshments. The younger brother of the great orator felt honored to be included with these senior officers. When he arrived, Labienus's slaves were laying out the amphorae of wine and arranging the chairs for the guests. Other men trickled in and Labienus poured the Mulsum, a mixture of wine and honey   only served on special occasions.

The men relaxed into their seats, it had been a long and hard day.

"Enjoy yourselves, we have earned a small banquet at the very least; I hope you like my special treat." Labienus was most charming, at least to ones who heeded him. And it was a feast, at least to the army men who had been away from Rome all summer. All of the men there were patricians of Rome, young men who would someday be Senators, or more.

The slaves served them platters of apricots and nuts, several kinds of special cheeses, and the finest white bread. The loaves were hot from the oven that Labienus kept with him, with bits of garlic and a generous topping of butter. This would have been a feast in itself for the men, but there was more. Salted olives, dried grapes, and special little cakes. Labienus traveled with ten slaves, three of which did nothing but prepare his food and care for the little creatures.

There was other wine, some very pure from the slopes of Italy, and the men drank up. "Don't eat too much; I've got a special treat for you." Two of the Sicilian slaves brought in a brazier that was glowing with coals, and the third man brought in the cage of dormice.

Labienus was famous for his dormice; he took a colony of them every where he went and one of his slaves did nothing but care for them and make sure the population matched the occasional demand of his master. "The proper way gentlemen, or at least the way I like them."

The slave brought one out of the special cage. "They must be fresh," said the host. With a practiced flourish the cook popped off the head and eviscerated it, and quickly peeled off the skin; taking great care to not damage the delicate meat underneath. He then stuffed it with minced spiced pork, dipped the delicacy in honey, then rolled it in pounded pine nuts.

With that, he impaled the dormice on a skewer and lowered it carefully in the searing olive oil. After a few seconds, he presented the little delicacy to Labienus. A quick savor and then a bite, "Perfect. Proceed with the cooking. My friends, happiness to you and the Roman Senate."

* * * * *

The Centurion of the Thirteenth Legion stood on the wall as the Officer on Duty approached. "I wish they would quiet down; their stink is bad enough without the screeching and screaming."

"Yes sir, it is disagreeable but at least it keeps the Gauls awake." The Centurion turned after saluting and went to make his report. The Mandubii were starting to throw the bodies in the trench.

DAY 21

The Morini came out of the reeds at dawn. Before the Roman cavalry men could wake and react, the little men had killed the sentries and they were on them. Then just as quickly, they disappeared with eleven Roman bodies lying in the mud.

* * * * *

Later that morning, Caesar emerged from his tent to be greeted by the senior guardsman on duty.

"Sir, the officer on duty reported last night that the Gauls are stacking their dead in the trench. He didn't think it was important enough to wake you."

Caesar strode calmly to the first watchtower and ran up the steps. He was a lithe and active man, even compared to one much younger than he was. He took the legionary's salute and looked over the four hundred feet to the mass of Mandubii. After a few minutes, he turned and went back for his morning meeting.

"Are the men in order? I may make an inspection this afternoon. Let the word of it slip out, I don't want to embarrass my fighters but I expect them to be properly honed."

"It was a long day of drills yesterday, Caesar, but I'll let the rumor out to the Primus Pilas, that'll put them spitting and polishing." Delmonus curried favor at every opportunity. The other officers were used to that.

"Tomorrow we'll have trumpet and signal drills. I may change the order; the Gauls have been hearing the current ones so long they'll know them better than we do. Delmonus, will you see to that? Draw up a proposed new system for me." Caesar was not an unobservant man and he had his own sense of humor. "Anything else?"

Labienus asked, "General, do you want to do anything about them laying the bodies in the trench? I'm sure that the Gauls plan on using them as fill for when they try to cross."

"Let them." Caesar went into his private chambers.

* * * * *

"Are the ladders and hooks all ready?" Vercin had all the leaders assembled on the ground behind the main gate. "Do you each have your sector and your plan beyond the ditch?" All the men nodded. Most were in a fog from the night's drinking, but the ladders were finished.

"The men are anxious, Vercin, when can we go?" The question was asked every day, but Vercin answered it today for the first time.

"When I see Commius ride up on that hill over there." He turned and motioned for me to follow him. We walked the streets; "I don't know how much longer I can stand this, Cass. Some of the men want to make a suicide attack; they've had it and so have I."

* * * * *

The Romans were bringing in the last of their horses. The area between the two walls would give them their exercise, and allow them to be close by if the Gauls moved. There was no need for large patrols any more; the few patrols that were out had orders to report in at the first sign of any movement on the roads. The horses must be fit and rested when the attack came.

The men were polishing their armor and sharpening their swords. They were veterans; they knew what difference an edge could make. Cellus was watching Quintus buff his shield and chain mail with the river sand. Some of the men were brushing off each other's tunics; a couple of them were lying under the shade from the tent.

"You're all beautiful," Pexius giggled. His companion thought that was funny too; Quintus didn't even bother to look up. He was used to this prattle.

DAY 20

The elder druidae were alone in the forest. There were many people in the camp near the Nemetos, and there were matters to discuss. It was a clear and crisp morning, there in the trees. All the men had put blankets underneath themselves as they sat.

"Can you see what will happen, Draius?"

"No, I don't know what will happen, Clarus, but I don't feel good about things. Caesar is too complacent. Maybe he thinks that Commius and the Aedui aren't coming; maybe he's right. I think the Belgae left for Alesia, but I can't tell that for sure. Gaul is a big cloud to me now; maybe I've gotten to old to have the power anymore. Maybe the day of the druidae is over. I wish that we could have kept Vercassivellaunus with us, his potential was limitless and he would have finished his training by now and taken my place; but, he is where he wants to be."

The druidae rose as if by a silent command and went to the towering oak; they formed a circle around it and silently meditated.

*****

Thousands of Mandubii were dead, and thousands more were almost the same. The ones that could threw the bodies in the trench; that grisly work went on all day. When the last were laid the ones left gathered along the edge of the grave to say goodbye; that's when the Roman ballistae began the barrage.

*****

Caesar called a general staff meeting at noon that day. Not just the usual top generals, but the supply officers, and the artillery men, the physicians and all that were in a position of authority.

"Is there anything left to do? Everything must be prepared before the other Gauls get here. First, the artillery."

"General, the weapons are all ranged, the trenches in front as well as the outer one. The markings are laid, and even alternate ones should we have to reinforce other sectors."

"What about ammunition?" Caesar asked.

"Each machine is stocked; each tower has its piles of rock and arrows. Runners have been assigned and are practicing running up the stairs to reload. Baskets of the small rock are arranged for when the Gauls get to the inner trenches."

"The walls?" The artillery commander answered, "Scorpio are placed every twenty feet with plenty of their arrows next to them. We now change the drawstrings every morning, just in case they've weakened in the night. We can completely cover the length of the outer ditches and then contract the ballistae to the points of attack as they cross."

"Flarious, are you ready for casualties?" Caesar looked at Flarious, "Are your men prepared to speed those along who can't be helped?"

"Yes, Caesar, my attendants are trained and practiced. The surgery tents are well placed and supplied with saws and bandages. When the attacks start, we'll light our pyres for the limbs and bodies. We have all the medicines known to Rome and we'll save all we can."

"When their reinforcements start appearing I want food to be cooked and available. It'll be a long day's fight and I want my men kept strong. Place barrels of water and stacks of bread all around the walls. Delmonus, would you see to that?"

"I want all of you to tell your Centurions that they will personally inspect the armor and weapons of each man. No dull or nicked swords, no broken chain mail, and for the love of Mars make sure the pila are not warped! I don't want their rocks flying off into space when they're thrown. I don't know who was responsible for them at Gergovia but if it happens again I'm going to hang some armorers."

DAY 19

Boduognados and a great host of his warriors rode out of the land of the Nervii. The men wanted to go to the fight and so did he. If they rode hard, they would catch up with Commius before he left Bibracte; there would have to be some organizing and arguing there, there always was. Other tribes were marching; groups of men in the hundreds and the thousands were rushing to Bibracte to join. It would be glorious; that day they met the Romans.

* * * * *

Vercingetorix had ordered a final head count, but there was a mob scene behind the walls. "Get your men organized! I don't want them roaming all over Alesia sniffing in every cupboard and amphora!" He glared at the chiefs. "We've got a battle coming; this isn't a raid we're on. They can steal what the Mandubii left later, when the fighting's done."

* * * * *

I took my father home. There were still ways in and out of Alesia for small groups; as long as the Remi looked the other way, and it was a dark night. Gobanitio was old; and he was a beaten man. He needed to be with my mother and she needed him. We got to the farm about sunup and I fell into my old bed. At noon, my mother woke me, she had made my favorite foods and we got to talk as mother and son. When I left that night, my parents were packing to go to the forest, where the cellar was.

When I got back to Alesia, I was told that Vercingetorix had left in the predawn hours with some warriors of the Arverni. They were attacking the hilly area that we felt were the weak spot in the Roman lines. It was foolish of him to go; if he were killed, our war would be over. However, he made it back, with a lot of the men who had left. But not all.

* * * * *

Inside the Roman camp, the preparations for battle continued. The Roman Legionary carried into combat his gladius and two pila. He wore the chain armor and carried his shield

223

and had a helmet, usually dented and scarred, for they outlived the men and were passed on to new recruits. Each man was responsible for his equipment being in perfect condition for battle. Most of the veterans needed no urging; they were all experienced at surviving. When a soldier went into combat, he carried a canteen of water and some bread for it could be an all day fight.

Most battles weren't continuous for everyone; they would fight and then pull back and let the next man to assume his place in the line. At Alesia, there would be very few lulls though, the Legions were heavily outnumbered and all would could fight would be continuously thrown into combat. The men knew this, they could count; but a legionary lived for the day like this and he was ready when it did.

* * * * *

Caesar stood on the wall with Labienus; the field of battle was set. There were thousands of corpses lying to the far side of it. The Gauls behind their wall would come over the dead to get to the Roman barricade. They would come; Caesar would count on that. The two generals walked the length and breadth of what was left of Rome in Gaul. Caesar wasn't unhappy; his men were ready.

DAY 18

I could see things clearly now. Draius would send the young novitiates to the isles. They would carry the news of our situation to our cousins there. They would stay to carry on for us in the ways of the druidae of Gaul. The line had to be unbroken. I could see Ladia and the boys; she was playing with them in the forest. They had their swords with them and she showed them how their father used his. They would be safe from all this; they would return some day, when Rome was gone.

Our men were ready for what would come; we would meet in victory at the Roman camp or we would meet somewhere else in our next lives. A Keltoi warrior lived for this.

* * * * *

Vercin and Gerromir went with me to Brossix's house. We were old friends now, the ones who had started all of this. Sedullos was out there somewhere killing Romans; we knew that. Commius was coming; we knew that too. When there was a war, our people found it.

Mirandia fed us what she had. Meals were sparse now and very plain, but we could make it for a few more days. It wouldn't be too long now. There weren't many horses left, they had been in bad shape when our cavalry left and provided the little meat we got. Most everything that breathed in Alesia was someone who carried a sword; or else like Mirandia, the women who wouldn't leave.

The screams from outside were fewer now, and weaker. Those poor people were a sacrifice to the liberty of Gaul; there was no other choice. Vercin was a sacrifice too, and I guess all of us were. We talked about the way it had started, us old friends. We had been reckless, and maybe foolish, but we all felt pride anyway. If we died here, we'd die as men who had fought.

I didn't tell the others what I was seeing now; I couldn't change the future. The gods did what they wished to do.

* * * * *

Far away from Alesia, the slave market in Norbo was busy. The latest shipload of captives had left for Rome and the sheds and barracks had to be washed out. They were a breeding ground for disease as people came and went. The attendants had done this before, many times. Buckets of water had to be carried in and then the scrubbing began. Thousands of new ones would be arriving soon, it was said. There were already caravans on the roads from Gaul.

* * * * *

The young druidae got on the ship. They had never left Gaul before; in fact, most of them knew only their homes before they had left for Nemetos; and then just the forest home since. The ocean was terrifying; but Draius had told them to do this. They would be with their like in Britannia.

* * * * *

We walked Alesia, and we planned. We spoke with our war chiefs. They showed us where they would cross and attack. There were lots of ladders and bundles of sticks lying next to the gates; we'd start slipping them out the night when we saw Commius. In the meantime, there needed to be a fire. We took pitch and oil down to the trench. The bodies in them had to be burned; our men couldn't walk on them when they went across. The smell in the air was unbearable. The few Mandubii left weren't much help; they just mostly lay there and watched us.

DAY 17

"Urdus, these are your orders." Antonius was the overall commander of the cavalry; both Roman and the auxiliaries and the Germani. The German chief stood there and listened, then he walked away, back to his camp. His leaders were there at his tent when he came back.

"Caesar doesn't need us any more; he didn't even give me the respect of telling me himself. They told me for us to go look for the others, the ones who are coming. Then we're supposed to fight them for Caesar while his men sit here and wait for that town to fall. They'll get everything in it while we're riding all over Gaul looking for death. We'll leave at dawn; we won't be coming back."

* * * * *

We got into the Roman camp last night, but we didn't stay long. They rallied fast. We had wanted to harass and then get out and we did; we left some tents burning behind us though; and some dead Romans. I saw Brossix cut a Roman in half with that big sword of his; I guess the Roman wasn't one of his old friends.

* * * * *

There was cause for celebration today. Some of the Venetti had found a cellar full of food. I guess it had been the hidden supply of the Mandubii. I don't know how they found it because it was cleverly hidden, but those men had ways. Now, every house was being torn up looking for others like it and the men were in such moods that we couldn't control them when they did find one. They just sat down and gorged themselves on anything they could eat, even raw grain. They were animals now. We had to turn them loose soon; I was taking some of them out that night on another raid. I knew where a group of Roman workers were staying; outside the outer wall.

* * * * *

Draius watched little Gobanitio and Celtillus play. Ladia sat nearby with her head against a tree, and her eyes closed.

227

"Draius, what will happen? When will Vercin come for us?"

"When it's over, dear girl. When it's all over; soon. Which one of your sons will be the king? Can you tell yet?"

* * * * *

Vercin and I finished our sword practice; not that we needed it, but it made the time pass. Brossix had stuck a big post in the ground and covered it with leather and we slashed and hacked at it until our shoulders ached and we laughed together as we had when we were young. I missed being young. It had not been that long ago when we rode the hills of Arvernia and hunted the stag, the boar, and sometimes even a farm girl. It had been good when we were young princes.

Ladia was one of those maidens, and Vercin kept her to be his princess. And she was one, even then. She grew up on a farm near us and we passed her house every day one summer. Vercin would sit erect on his horse and act as if he didn't notice her, but I knew differently. I could see his red face. He came for her a couple of years after I left; it wasn't unexpected.

I had found no love, until now. I loved war. I loved the fear on a man's face when I rode at him; when he knew he would die.

DAY 16

Commius and all his forces had gathered at Bibracte; together with the Aedui, there were over sixty thousand of them now, a lot of them riders. He had started sending patrols ahead; first one group and then the next day another. The Belgae had the blood look in their eyes, and now the others were beginning to get it too. They'd all be at Alesia in a few days and six years of hate and frustration rode with them.

The Germans rode out of the Roman fort. There were almost four hundred of them and they rode north toward Commius. There was nothing in their way, they had already killed and burnt it all. When they began to see riders, they went into the hills and waited. Urdus sat in the trees and watched the Keltoi outriders. He wanted to know how many were behind them and to do that he had to wait. So, he waited. An army moved slowly, much slower than a few men do, and then he'd have decisions to make.

* * * * *

The drills went on; they never stopped in Caesar's army and this time they'd be defending a wall, one of the rare times they did this. It was no difference to these men; just the same swords, shields, and blood, like it always was. Then they could go home. Richer than when they'd left; the ones that got home anyway.

* * * * *

Quintus and Rounia were in a fight. They pulled Quintus off the man before he could stomp him again; he looked like he would kill. It didn't happen very often, normally the men who shared a tent and a meal wouldn't come to that, but the old warrior had had enough and he had beaten the man senseless and then gone to work with his boots before Pexius and the others could grab him. The Centurion watched, then turned and walked away. Men in the Roman army had their own way.

* * * * *

Caesar sat in his chair; the Greek slave was shaving him and Caesar felt good. The men were dangerously close to that fighting edge where they didn't care anymore; they were not afraid or thinking of home. They were just thinking about killing and killing until there wasn't anyone left to kill. This time would be different. This would be the end of Gaul and he'd go home to his dessert; and he would finally be rich.

He owed a lot of money; more than a lot. Crassus had funded him and had been patient but that wouldn't be needed anymore. He'd take enough gold and slaves home with him to pay his debts and live like a king forever. King forever was a good thought. Rome would be at his feet. His entire life led to this final triumph and now he would rule an empire.

DAY 15

Cato and Pompey met privately in Pompey's mansion. War had been good to Pompey, even if he had been rich before. He had slaves that did nothing but prepare his food and dozens of others to clean and wait on him; he missed Cornelia though.

"Sit, my friend. I'm not in a hurry for a change and it's time to talk of specifics." Cato sat, but that didn't relieve his apprehension. Speaking of specifics could be a serious business. People died for it, and Pompey was the most powerful man in Rome and like Caesar was adored by the people. Pompey had given the people riches and conquests, and Caesar spoke to them of the sweetness of democracy.

"What will Caesar want if he conquers Gaul, Cato? I know what I want for Rome and I think I know what you want, but those thieving plotting Senators of ours have their own ambitions that never end. It would be amusing, in another time, to watch them tussle with Caesar, but that might mean the end of the Rome we see. So what will Caesar want?"

"Why he wants to be king, Pompey. It's as simple as that."

"And how will he achieve that?"

"I don't know, but can't you feel and see it coming?" Cato was often called the only honest man in Rome; he was also the bluntest.

"So what will you do?" asked Pompey.

"I will do anything I must, General, to prevent that. And I hope you will too. Our republic is very fragile right now; those greedy men on those hills have put our Rome in a tenuous position and a man who has reached the pinnacle that Caesar has, can with one more victory, send what we have built here in Rome crashing down. We are that close to seeing this happen. A man with that much power and the love of the people will destroy what Rome is.

"I didn't," said Pompey.

As he went home that night, Cato thought to himself, "That's what I'm counting on, you arrogant bastard."

* * * * *

The men behind the walls of Alesia sat and waited. There were no women and there was no drink, and the sullenness was building. There were fights every day. Men fought at the wells, they fought at the planning sessions, they fought other tribes, and if strangers weren't around, they fought with each other. They were hungry, and not nearly tired enough. Something must happen soon or the snapping point would be reached and then it would all be over.

"Vercin, some of the chiefs want to attack now. They don't think much in the best of times and now they're reaching the point of throwing themselves on that barricade of Caesar. If we lose unity it's all over."

"I know Cass, I know. What can we do? We'll be massacred if we try to scale those walls without Commius on the other side. I wish I could put them to work at something, but they wouldn't; they're on to that now. There's nothing to do until we attack."

Wallaurus, war chief of the Pictones, stood on the wall and planned his advance. He'd studied the land over and over again. Right there was where he would put his bundles and timbers. His men could cross ten abreast and then they'd begin the run. They'd be carrying a lot of ladders and lengths of rope, and the hooks were heavy too. But most would make it, in some shape or another. The problem would be after they crossed the trench. They wouldn't have the bundles to help them over the next two, and one was full of water. They'd have to throw their ladders across them and go over that way. The air would be thick with every thing the Romans could throw at them. Wallaurus absentmindedly stroked his red hair. It wasn't braided like it usually was; he had loosened the braids days ago. A Keltoi warrior fought with the pride of his manliness proudly displayed.

DAY 14

"He's been standing in that same spot for a week now. Do you think he has his route picked out?"

"Of course he does, Rommus; that man has been fighting this battle in his mind for that week you mentioned. Over and over in his mind. He's seen his tribe rushing across the trench a thousand times. He's seen them pick up their ladders and rush across that field to the next one." Labienus told the young tribune.

"Which way will he come?"

Labienus stared hard at Rommus. "In a straight line."

The Roman Centuries came to their armorers' area one by one. Each Legion had a group that tested and inspected the weapons. The sharpening stones were constantly moving as the swords were edged. There were grim men standing in those lines; they were ready for what was to come. Far past being ready.

Every Immune in Caesar's army had his job. Weapons, armor, uniforms, medicals, farriers and on and on. They worked steadily to prepare the fighting men for this battle. Then, when it came, they'd pick up their own weapons and go to the fight. Everyone in the Legion would fight that day. They'd win, or they'd die; they all knew that.

* * * * *

For thirteen years, Brossix served the Roman Legions. There would be men there that he knew; men that he'd fought with and ate with and looted and raped with, but it didn't matter any more. He was a Gaul again and he would kill the Romans that had come to his land.

Mirandia served him a bowl of porridge. She had crumbled up some bread and mixed it with the milk from the last goat. They had an onion too. Tomorrow they'd begin to eat the goat; and after that, she didn't know. She had met her man two years before he took his retirement and came home to Gaul. She had been working on the edge of the Roman army for most all her life; and had known many men and hardships, but this was the worst. It was more than gloomy behind the walls of Alesia.

Vercin and I stood on the wall and watched the Romans drill. It never ended.

"That's why they win, Cass, that's all they know, winning. They never stop preparing."

* * * * *

Commius was moving. He had his army now, but he had to get them to Alesia and the roads were few and narrow. He was moving much slower than he wanted to. I am coming, Vercingetorix, I'm coming, he thought, as he rode along. The tribe of German warriors watched them from the trees on the hill as they came. They watched, and when the Gauls got closer, they moved to another hill or another forest and watched as more came down that road.

DAY 13

The Roman Signifer was the standard bearer for the Legions and their units. One, called the Aquilifer carried the eagle of the Legion. Below him was the Signifer who carried the standard of the Century or Cohort. A Draconarius carried the one of each cavalry unit attached to a Legion.

These standards served as not only the pride of a unit but the rallying point in battle. They were sacred to the honor of the Roman unit and were essential in the commotion of war. A man could look around and find where his officers wanted him to be because the signifer was an extension of the officer in charge.

Commands were given by horns. The cornu was curved and could rest on a man's shoulders and signaled the location of the standard, and announced the movement of the body and its senior officers. Another horn called a trumpet signaled the charge or retreat of men in battle without the movement of the established position. The sound of the cornu told the legionary where the core of their location was established and the trumpet told them to attack from that position or to retreat to it.

A third horn, called a buccina, was shaped like a sea shell. It was exclusive to the general in charge. It announced his presence or the presence of those with his authority.

These signals and sounds were very simple but were effective methods used to command the Roman soldier, and they trained and drilled to these constantly. The key to the Roman Legion was its discipline and cohesiveness. When the officers got their men in position there were other commands for formations and basic movement.

The men of Caesar practiced constantly their individual skills and their unit movements. Everything was constructed to get the proper personnel into a position where their individual power was combined into an overall force that was stronger than its individual parts.

We'd never have that unity. When we fought, every man just went at an enemy with his full fury; not knowing if the man beside and behind him was an enemy or a friend. This was the way of the Keltoi; we weren't afraid of death. A warrior who isn't afraid of death is a terrifying presence; as long as he was stayed alive.

The Roman drills continued. The Immunes shod the horses, sharpened the swords, and organized the placement of barrels of water. The medicals prepared the bandages and organized the herbs they used and practiced stretcher bearer drills. The supply officers put the food in locations that could be quickly accessed. Caesar played with his plaster models; but they weren't just models of Alesia. He made others; of Spain and Asia and Africa and there were colored figures representing armies. Two of those armies even faced each other along a river in Italy.

DAY 12

Gerromir had plans. When this battle was over, he was going to retrieve Darla and her daughter and go home. Home for him was the land that faced the sea, the land of the Venetti. His people were fishermen and sailors and traders; and some were even described in the shipping lanes between Gaul and Britannia as predators. He was going back to his life but he didn't plan on fishing.

He had commanded a ship of war until the Romans came. They had fought but the Romans had won and when the Romans won against there was total annihilation. Gerromir's home was destroyed, his city burned to the ground; his wife and his two sons lay buried in it. After five years as a slave, he had managed to escape by killing the Roman guards who thought he was their friend.

He'd go back now; he had a family again. The Romans would be gone and he would be a seaman like a Venetti should be. Today he had other things to do. Things that would help him kill the men who had killed his family and tribesmen.

*****

We knew the weakness of the Roman fortifications. It was the area broken by the hills; it would be hard for the Legions to keep their cohesiveness there, and our warriors could attack and start killing. They knew their role; find a Roman and kill him and then find another and kill him. We had more men than Caesar did and if we could keep him busy on the walls, we at one side and Commius on the other could pierce that Roman defense. If we got in those walls, our numbers would overwhelm him, Roman discipline or not. It would be warrior on warrior then.

I would lead that attack. I had no ladders or grappling hooks, just men who had no fear. It suited me. Riders were beginning to signal from the hills; they had seen signs of the army of Commius. We didn't know how near he was, but now we knew he was on his way. The shouts of our people had once again passed from mountain to mountain and valley to farm and on to the hills surrounding Alesia.

We were mostly quiet now, and waited. Vercingetorix had sent the tribes, one by one, to wash and prepare their battle dress. They loosened their hair and made ready. We always did this before a battle; we wanted to look our best. This seemed to take the edge off the temper of our army; they were refreshed and combed. They were Keltoi warriors in all their glory. This seemed to settle them down. It would be days yet before we needed them to turn vicious again.

DAY 11

Urdus's scouts began to come in to his camp. Small groups of German riders had been looking for the Gauls and were shadowing them as they gathered in the fields and on the roads of Gaul. Urdus himself was camped on a mountain where he could see the movements from a distance but his men had been closer; assessing and counting.

"The roads are full, Urdus, more than the roads. The Gauls are coming from everywhere, crossing the fields and converging toward this valley. There will be a sea of Gauls in a couple of days." The warrior named Goch had ridden with Urdus for a long time. "And it's not only farmers and villagers coming. It's men on horses carrying spears and swords and men on foot carrying anything they can find to fight with."

Urdus sat and thought. When his Germans swooped down on a town, the men in it ran. If these same men were coming now carrying axes, hoes, and scythes, that meant they were ready to fight. Ready to fight the might of the Roman Empire. "We'll eat now and rest, then take me to see this army."

The sky on the horizon was dark with the dust of moving men and animals. The hills and the valleys looked like they were shaking as the constant blurring of movement came up and down each.

Two hours before sunset, Urdus's German horsemen rode toward the east. The east was where the Rhine was, and Germania. They had come for loot, not to die for Rome; they were going home.

* * * * *

Vercin called all the generals together. All the tribes were represented. "Commius is coming; we don't know how many but he promised two hundred and fifty thousand. It's a matter of a few days now, can your men last?" No one said anything because each would have said the same thing. Their men were hungry, more than hungry, but each shared the pain of his brother now. Besides, there wasn't anything left to drink or steal.

239

"Vercassivellaunus is going to meet them; we all know our roles and it's important that Commius knows what we want him to do, and when. Cass, you speak for me and all these men. Tell Commius, the Aedui, and the others that you have the command. Take Gerromir with you; if there are any arguments, kill the man who doubts you. Take my standard of the king of the Arverni to prove you represent me, and if that's not enough use your swords to prove the point. I don't have the inclination for pettiness now. Do you hear me, Gerromir? Cass is the leader of the Gauls outside those Roman lines. But if his good nature takes over him, kill those men for me."

We were to ride out before dawn. We had to be a small group to get through the Roman lines. I asked the Horned One to guide me.

DAY 10

Caesar walked the Roman lines every day. He'd stop and talk to the men; some of them he knew by name. He had his slaves bring food at midday to wherever he was and he'd sit and share his food with the men nearby. He talked to them about the glory of Rome, what it represented, and how he would change things when they returned home.

"The symbol of Rome is the letters SPQR, as you all know. That means 'The Senate and the People of Rome.' I don't like that symbol. Rome is Rome; there is not two Romes, or even one Rome with two kinds of people in it. We're all Romans. Your blood is on the ground in Gaul, and it's the same color as the blood of the Roman Senate.

"We'll go home and we'll go home together and we will know that we conquered Gaul and the fierce men who live in it. Gaul will then be a part of Rome. You and I have conquered it and you and I will rule it; any of the Senate who wish to can come here and fight with us. But the might of the Roman Legion is for all of Rome, not just the few."

The men listened; they had followed him and he'd never failed them and they wouldn't fail him now. When he commanded, they would go anywhere he told them.

PAT MIZELL

DAY 9

I found Commius my second day out. It wasn't hard; I just had to look for the man sitting highest in his saddle, riding harder than any others around him. I had been seeing riders for a day now, and when I asked about him, they pointed behind. He's coming, they said, and with a lot of men.

When I rode up to his group, he let out a roar, and then all the Gauls began to roar too. We had united at last. We didn't sit there long; we could talk that night. We just rode south. For the first time in weeks, I felt like a Keltoi warrior again. It felt good.

That evening we camped early because tomorrow we'd go to Alesia and there was much to plan. Commius and the Nervii king named Boduognados sat with Gerromir and me, and the leaders of the Aedui. I told them what Vercin wanted and there was no argument from anyone. They knew why they were there and that's all they cared about. Tomorrow we would kill or cast Rome from our lands.

I gave the war chiefs their assignments and drew the Roman encampment on the ground for them. There sat Alesia, with a circle of Romans over ten miles long surrounding us. Sixty thousand Romans sat behind that line and then another circle of battlements and walls ran around them and Alesia that was fourteen miles long. That would be our responsibility.

"How many men are with you Commius?" I asked.

"I'm not sure but there are twenty thousand of us on horse here now and many more coming behind us, both horse and foot. I guess we won't know for sure until we stop at Caesar's wall, if we have to stop."

"We will; Vercin wants us all there before the first attack. When we hit them, it will be at the same time; all of yours and all inside Alesia hitting the Roman camp together, as one."

He nodded, all the chiefs did, and Gerromir and I enjoyed the first real food and drink in weeks as we sat around that fire of our friends that night. The next morning we rode to Alesia.

PAT MIZELL

DAY 8

When our army started to appear on the ridge tops and hillsides, the jubilation within Alesia erupted as nothing ever had before, at least in my eyes. I had been there most of the time and I knew what those men had gone through; and now it would be over. The men who had wanted to throw themselves at Rome for the last week would get their wish. Men like Vercin and me, who had suffered through the years of planning and building and waiting had reached our greatest ambition. All of Gaul would be united against the greatest army in the world.

Vercin felt that if we defeated Caesar, or destroyed him, Rome would not be back. We ignored any other thought; this was Gaul's day. The walls of Alesia must have been built right, for it seemed like every one of our sixty thousand men were standing on them. The teeming hills around it matched their cheering and taunting at the legions of Caesar; we had them at last at a place of our choosing with the strength to overcome the might of the Roman Legions.

Commius's men kept riding and running along the skyline; I sat on my horse and watched them, and I watched my brothers inside Alesia; and I watched Julius Caesar's army. It was the greatest feeling of my life. Commius sat beside me looking like a god of war; towering, brutal, and quivering with the smell of the battle ahead. First though, we had to make the final plans. I had arranged before I left a signal that would tell Vercin where to meet us, and that night I lit the fire that showed him the way to the secret place.

He came in late, sneaking through the Roman encirclement with Gerromir and two tribal leaders who represented the thirty-something inside. After the greetings, food, and drink, we bedded down for a few hours before our dawn meeting.

The plans had long been worked out but all of our armies had to follow them precisely; we knew Caesar would have his plans too, but this wouldn't be complicated; just hundreds of thousands of men throwing themselves at each other. We had to do that at the right time and place; we were facing the greatest army in the world, and the greatest general.

Commius, Vercin, two Aedui generals, our two, and I sat down at first light. Gerromir, at Vercin's instructions rode the lines of the Gauls; Vercin wanted to know what we actually had; but it would have to be enough; there were no more for Gaul to give. We made our plan that day. It took awhile, but we did it. We outnumbered the Roman army, but they had the walls and the ballistae. A lot of us would die in a few days.

Vercin left late that day; he had to sneak back into the city and give his final orders. I didn't go with him. It broke my heart not to go, but I had my assignment. Late that night, he met with the chiefs in Alesia and they began making their final plans. Most had been set for days, but one unexpected thing did come out. Vercin told the guards of the storehouses to divide all the food left into three rations. The men had been near starvation for the last two weeks and Vercin wanted them to regain their strength. Everything in Alesia would be gone in three days. On the fourth, we'd be eating Roman food.

DAY 7

"The red-haired chief came early this morning, Caesar. Him and the other ones we've been watching for the last few weeks. They came to the spots they always do, then at the same time they all left the wall. They haven't been back all day." Labienus was sitting alone with Caesar in the command tent.

"Well, we know where they're coming to, Labienus, but do they know that we know? I doubt it, but even if they do, it's too late to change. Start putting out the locators tonight. The men that place them will have to live in that trench until the Gauls come so they need to take enough food and water to last them, but it will be the day after tomorrow, I'm sure. They can't be ready by morning and can't wait any longer than the next."

Caesar's last piece of strategy was put in place that night. He was sure he knew where our men would cross the trench, and from those crossing spots, he knew our warriors would then come straight at the fortification, but he also knew that we would start putting our bundles of sticks and branches in those spots at night, hopefully unobserved. Caesar sent men into the trench, not a lot that could be spotted, but enough to watch and locate the crossing spots. Then they put little red flags inside the little lip that he had left on the Roman side of the trench. They were small flags, but could be seen by his artillery men while hidden from us.

Hundreds of ballistae would be aimed at those crossings and then shifted to other marks that were likely to be used in a head on attack. Our Gauls didn't know any other way than head on. We would be met by a hailstorm of boulders and rocks and then the thousands of arrows from the Scorpio. Then we'd meet one hundred and twenty thousand of the pila before we got to the sixty thousand Roman swords. But we would come.

We would rush out of all five of Alesia's gates as one. Each man would have a bundle or an end of a ladder in his hands; the sixty thousand of us carrying the means to get to sixty thousand Roman swords that waited behind four hundred feet of ditches and stakes and traps and missiles. Vercin stood at the wall late that day; I could see his blond hair from my hill. He just stood there and looked toward Caesar. It would all end soon.

DAY 6

We sat that day, most of it, as did the Romans and the men in Alesia. Caesar's slaves and our men both brought wood and made pyres, for today we would make our sacrifices to our gods, as they would to theirs. Men were ready. Were the gods? Had they decided our fates yet? Did Roman gods and Keltoi gods meet and make plans too? Did they conspire and decide the outcome? It didn't matter; we would do what we would do.

The Legions of Rome assembled; they could not all come to the same place but as one in spirit and near to each other in physical presence it was the same. As the executioner's swords swung, each man made his own prayer to the main gods of Rome and to his own personal gods that he favored. As the oxen and the new lambs were placed on the pyres the men solemnly watched, and when the fires were ignited the roar of nearly sixty thousand men filled the fields of Alesia. Caesar and all the major officers of Rome rode in procession around the fires and the cheers went on and on.

The Gauls watched from the hills and the walls of Alesia.

There were no goats, lambs, or cattle inside Alesia, just men. There were thirty six tribes inside those walls and thirty six men stepped forward. They were the bravest of the brave. Slowly they walked around them kinsmen, saying goodbye; and then began their walk to the gigantic stack of timber center of the city.

As each stepped forward and allowed his hands to be tied, the respective tribes began their chants and war cries and the roar of the Rome army was matched by the roars of Gaul. Thirty six roars became one.

DAY 5

We could hear the Gauls inside Alesia singing our chants and songs and praising our gods; and we echoed them. Keltoi warriors worked themselves into a battle frenzy that would only stop when the enemy was dead, or they were. This went on most of the day. The next day, we would fight.

The Romans didn't drill that day; they rested. They sat and sharpened their swords one last time. They filled their canteens with water after they had emptied them of the wine. Food was cooked and set by the walls and barrels of water and pitch to be lighted. Mounds of rocks sat next to the towers that were placed every eighty feet for miles across that field. The groups of men assigned to them were there by the towers. The ensigns of the cohorts stood by their places behind the wall.

The physicians were prepared. They would have a busy day. They had pyres of wood too, there by their medical tents. Men's limbs and bodies would be thrown in these fires. The Roman generals set in Caesar's tent late that day; there wasn't much more to discuss. The final inspections had been made and they just mostly sat and talked. There was no planning left. Just the killing and the dying.

Caesar rode the lines that day on his white stallion. His armor gleamed; he was the perfection of Rome. He'd stop and get down at every unit's standard and talk to his men. His men. The men who loved him and followed him on days like this. He was their god.

That night the ten legions of Romans sat by their fires and waited for the morning, as did the tribes of Gaul.

DAY 4

We struck at dawn. Commius led almost ten thousand horsemen down that hill and filled the three mile front facing the Roman camp. They started their trot. The Aeduian generals then led their infantry down to the bases of the hills and waited; I looked toward Alesia and imagined my brother standing there watching too. Then Julius Caesar accepted our challenge.

His cavalry poured out the gates of the Roman encampment and the horsemen of the Belgae met them. If there is anything that is more majestic than nearly twenty thousand men on horses meeting on a field of battle, I hope I get to see it someday. I sat on my horse from atop the nearest hill and watched that battle; the day that Gaul finally threw its men against the might of Rome.

I watched as the gates of Alesia opened and the men rush out of it. They filled the ditch they had dug with bundles of sticks and sacks of dirt and stomped around in war fury while they awaited the command that would send them across those hundreds of feet to meet Rome; waiting for Commius and the Aedui to reach the wall. That time never came.

Commius's men charged and retreated, then charged again. The Roman cavalry met every charge with their own and then when they came after him the second time, our ambush struck. Commius had taken archers and slingers with him, hidden among his horse; and the Romans rode face first into our missiles. We thought we had them then; the Romans retreated in disarray, but when we tried to press the advantage, they rallied and stopped us.

This went on all afternoon. Savage men from the Belgae tribes and others from the north of Gaul threw themselves at the Roman horsemen and then the Romans would come back at them. Thousands of men lay dead and maimed on that ground but the armies kept fighting. They would charge and rest, then receive a charge and it went back and forth; and then Caesar struck the blow that ended the day. Everyone was exhausted, the

Romans too, and it only took a small tilt on the field of battle to make everyone call it a day.

Caesar had watched all of this from his wall. It would take me a long time to realize it, but he wasn't in the least worried that day, he was just receiving the best that Gaul had and we didn't even maim his legions. When he had watched enough and seen enough men die, he opened his gate and sent out the Remi and their barbarian German allies that rode with them in a concentrated attack on our archers. The Germans slaughtered them while we rode around confused and disoriented from sudden attack.

That ended the battle; the remaining horsemen of Commius and the infantry on the hills went back to their camps, and the men of Alesia left that ditch and retreated to the sheltering walls of that city. We all retreated, except for the thousands of dead that lay on that plain. We had fought hard and bravely but we saw it wasn't going to be as easy as Commius thought.

DAY 3

Gaul had fought as Gaul always did that day; we had to find another way. Gerromir came to our camp that night and sat with me and we talked; the next morning we gathered and made a new plan. It took us a while, we had to argue and threaten, but then my friend left when the shadows of dusk first appeared to tell Vercingetorix what we had decided.

Before he left, we sat on the hilltop and watched the Romans gather their dead. They took them to the main gate of the fortress and stacked them into piles that they burned. We watched this, and we looked at the dead of Gaul lying on that field. We watched the wounded Belgae trying to move and the wounded horses twitching and pawing the air and we listened to the screams of the dying.

We had to take those ballistae away from them somehow, so we'd attack at night. If they couldn't see our movements across the field, we might make it to the walls and have our fight there, where the will of the warrior would count. We watched them all day and planned our assault. When the signal from us came, Vercin would bring out his men and we'd hit that Roman camp at one time. If in the darkness we weren't picked off by their artillery, then we could overwhelm them on their ramparts. At least we thought so. We went down there at midnight and it all began again.

When we stormed our side of the fortress, the Romans were blind; all they could do was fire those scorpio into the darkness and hope to hit something. They did; a lot of us went down from those arrows but a lot of us made it to the wall. We saw that we could win; we could feel it. We could see the confusion and fear in the Romans eyes so we lit the signal fire and Vercin led his men out the gates of Alesia.

We almost punched through on our side, but two of the Roman generals quickly pulled men from areas that weren't under attack and stopped us. Vercin's men got mired down in the stakes and traps and were sitting targets for the scorpio. The

Roman artillerymen didn't have to see us after all, they knew where we would be. Their weapons were ranged at those spots. Finally, near dawn, we withdrew.

It is impossible in so few words to describe the ineptness of our leaders compared to the professional officers of Rome. War to a Kelt was simple; we grabbed our swords and jumped on our horses and one tribe charged another until one was tired of the killing. We knew nothing. Every simple tactic we tried was easily countered by the experiences men of the legions who saw everything and were trained and drilled into stopping anything.

I think I finally realized then that we could not win. Somehow, if we couldn't get our overwhelming numbers of men face to face with the outnumbered Romans; we could never beat them. We had learned from the last two years that unless we slaughtered them, they would never leave Gaul. We had one thing left to try.

DAY 2

Commius, Sedullos, and I sat in a cloud of gloom. It was all our war now; some of the chieftains had left with their tribes during the night. The Aedui were trickling out of camp this morning and Vercin was powerless where he was. He had tried twice now to break out but the Roman defenses had sent him back each time. We had a method of signaling but he had no solution. It was up to those left here in the hills to do whatever was done.

For a month I had sat on those walls and watched the Romans put up their defenses. Vercingetorix and the others knew exactly what they had to do, there were no hidden secrets; we just couldn't overcome the trenches and traps and artillery. I only knew one thing left to try.

Two rivers ran by Alesia; Caesar's largest trench went from one to the other in a north south line. To the west, about four hundred feet away were the traps and smaller trenches, and the Roman barricade. At the north end of the barricade, a series of little hills and ravines didn't allow a perfect Roman wall to be built there. Caesar had put up what obstacles he could and heavily manned that spot with two legions. It was the only thing that we hadn't tried.

If we could break in there, we would be inside the Roman walls; and there was only one way to do that, by storming it. We made plans. I would take all the infantry left with us and at night go down our ridges to the far side of the hill that looked over that weak point. We would rest then and wait. When the sun reached its zenith, Commius would take all his riders across the plain in an attack from that side. Vercin would lead his men out of Alesia; neither would make it to the walls but my hope was that those attacks would give me the time to storm those little fortifications. If we could break in, we would roll up the Roman flanks without that awful artillery in our faces.

This would be our last hope. A lot of our army had gone home. Vercin's men were starved and unable to get across that plain, and Commius's horse couldn't break down those walls by itself. It was up to me; I took Sedullos with me and led tens of thousands of the most ferocious Gauls left out of those hills onto the far side of where my attack would come.

We made it there. We traveled through the darkness as quietly as thousands of men could and reached our lay up spot. All that morning the men rested and watered, and ate the bread and cold meat they had brought. At noon, we were ready. We heard Commius's horns first and then the thunder of ten thousand horses beating across that plain. Then Vercin's horn sent his starving survivors out the gates, and we started down to attack those two legions below us.

Our attack began and the Roman line bent; I thought we were going to make it then at their darkest moment reinforcement arrived. They slowed us and then Caesar himself led cavalry out; I could see his white horse and the scarlet clothing and shining armor that could only mean him. I saw them ride out as if they were going at Commius and disappeared in the haze of battle.

We fought, we killed, and we died, and then from behind us came Caesar leading thousands of cavalry straight at our backs. Men panicked and ran, and they died when those knights rode them down. Sedullos and I fought with the men who stayed with us but it was futile. I saw Sedullos die as he was hacked down and then trampled under the Roman horses' feet.

The men around me fought our way into the trees and hills. Roman riders were everywhere spearing and slashing our running remnant of an army and most of us died. I got away and reached our hidden camp, where the wounded lay and what few horses we had left were tethered. There wasn't anything left for us now. Our gods had decided.

DAY 1

I wasn't there, but Gerromir told me later of that last day in Alesia; before he made his escape. Vercin called the chieftains together and told them they could kill him and take his body to Caesar, or he would surrender himself to Caesar. They all knew what his fate would be, and theirs, but it was Caesar's decision now; and how.

Several of the old chiefs rode out the gate. Gerromir went over a back wall; he carried the brand of a Roman slave. Vercin went to Brossix's house. Brossix took his horse away as Vercin went with Mirandia. She brought water in and he bathed. Then he put on his finest clothes, those of an Arverni prince. Mirandia combed and brushed his hair and shaved all but his moustache. He wouldn't let her braid him though; he would go as a warrior, not a man at peace.

Brossix had curried and put the trappings of the Arverni on his horse and Vercin came out with the silver torque of a warrior around his neck and the great sword on his belt. He left Alesia as a god should look.

I had seen the other chiefs ride out. I sat on my horse and waited on the hill to the north. I saw my brother ride out of Alesia for the last time and he was every bit the king he was when he had ridden into Alesia those fifty-one days ago.

Caesar had erected his throne at the end of the plain; his generals stood behind him. Our surrendered chiefs stood to the side of them and the soldiers of Rome lined the way from the great trench to where Caesar sat. Vercin walked his horse down that lane and turned his head from side to side to look at the men of Rome; I think he saw me in the distance, but I never knew for sure.

He didn't ride as a beaten man but as the king of all he saw; the defiance was still on his face as he finally made it to Caesar's throne. He sat there for a minute, his armor glistening in the sun and the wind blowing his hair; then he threw his sword to the ground.

That was the day that Gaul died.

EPILOGUE

When I left that mountain, I looked like most of the people of Gaul. I was sunburned and gaunt, my hair was ragged, I had a scruffy beard, and my clothes were old and worn. I had a cheap knife and carried a sack with some meager country food and a blanket. Gesataia told me it wasn't uncommon to see men roaming and looking for work. Our farms had been devastated from the burnings, looting, and neglect, and many of the men who worked them had been killed or taken as slaves. That was over now; the end of the war had stopped the killing and slaving. It was time to rebuild. But I had other things in mind.

I walked that road that Rome had built; the one that so many of our people had walked down on the way to the slave markets of Narbo and wondered who of my friends had passed this way. Gesataia had told us that Caesar didn't take any Arverni or Aedui slaves; he claimed that he forgave us. That wasn't why, though; he wanted to divide us and leave resentment toward the leading tribes. Since I was Arverni, maybe I could feel somewhat safe. Roman patrols might harass me but there were no orders out and the Germans were gone.

People were generous as the days went by; they gave me what little they could spare and the crops were in the fields again and there was hope. I went to Brossix's farm first, he would know of things. But there was nothing there. It looked just like it did when he and Mirandia left months ago, except for some bugs, cobwebs, and rusting tools. I prowled around there looking for some sign or anything of use to me but there wasn't much except for a few scraggly beans growing in the weeds. I spent the night in the trees and then went home.

Arverni or not, I would have been a wanted man except Caesar thought he had captured me at Alesia. The man he thought was me had died before they found out differently. Gobanitio's and Vercin's farms were a few days journey away, and I had to be careful not to be seen by people who would know me; even if I were dead. I saw a few patrols on the journey and a slave caravan but I kept in the distance and had no trouble; maybe someday I would, I'd be ready then, but not now.

There was nothing on our farms. The buildings were burned down and nothing was alive there; I wasn't surprised but still I'd hoped. Like most farmers, my father had long along dug a cellar in the woods to hide in during raids; where no one but us knew of. I hoped my mother and father were still there. They were.

I buried them next to Vercin's father and mother that night. I stayed in our forest for a few days, scavenging what I could find, but I couldn't eat the food in the cellar and there wasn't anything else, so I had to leave. There was one thing I took though, my robe of the druidae. Then I left to join my kind and to find Ladia and the boys. I had promised Vercin.

I had made this trip to Nemetos many times, but this time it was different. I heard things that weren't there and saw things that weren't either. I stayed off the roads and kept to the forests. Things seemed so apparent to me; when I heard a bird chirp I immediately knew what tree it was in. I heard a rustling of leaves and sensed a rabbit under a bush. When I thought of Vercin, I could see him in a cage somewhere. And every step I took I seemed to be surrounded by a faint fog.

I spent five days on this journey, the same one I'd made in less than one before. When I reached our sacred place there in the forest, it had been destroyed. The huts that the druidae and the others had been living in were gone; burned and overgrown with weeds. Our sacred oak tree had been cut down, and bones were scattered everywhere about. It had been a good winter for the wolves. Darkness came and I made my bed in a thicket; the tomorrow would be a long day.

I poked around in the bones and tatters of clothing wondering which of my people they were. Underneath a pile of small bones, I found a ragged cloth bag; in it was a sword. A small sword like the ones Brossix had made for Vercin's boys. I left that morning with it tied to my waist and headed for the place where Draius had lived. He would be gone or dead but maybe he had left me a sign.

To my surprise, he was still living there. He told me that he had not been at Nemetos that day, and had never been back. He could nothing do but try to survive and hope one of us found him; not many knew where his home in the forest was. Draius told me that it had been the Remi. After Alesia, they had left and they were on their way back to Belgae, when an Aedui druida who had remained loyal to Caesar told them about our sanctuary. They had raided for slaves and plunder and out of hate for us.

It had not been much of a fight, Draius told me. The young druidae were in Britannia.

The people at Nemetos weren't warriors anyway. Ladia was not dead, though. He could see that. Of the little ones, he didn't know.

"She'll be in the south, Vercassivellaunus. The Remi have no use for slaves; they only take them to sell to the traders of Rome. Go to Rome, that's where you'll find her. I can see her sometimes; she's dressed well and occasionally smiles, but mostly just cries. Find the slave traders' records then you'll find her. The Romans always keep good records. But first there are some things you need to know."

I spent two months there with Draius and his wife. We resumed my training. "You have the power, Vercassive, I knew that when you were a child. It's awakening now but you must go through a period with one like me who has experienced this himself."

He worked with me constantly and told me of things that I had never known. Many druidae never reached this point, he said. Most didn't have the potential that I did or never developed it for some reason. I learned things that I needed to know and things I didn't want to know; certain responsibilities came with my awakening powers.

Draius took me deep into the forest and showed me one of the druidae's secrets. "This is our gold. It's been accumulated by us since the beginning of time and is yours to use as you see fit. There is enough here to buy cities, maybe even enough to buy Rome. You inherit this now from me; my power is going and yours is emerging. I knew when you were young that yours could far surpass me, but only time would tell if they did. They have. Take enough now to meet your needs on this journey and come back for more when you need it. I may not be here but it will be and it's your charge now."

Draius's wife made clothes for me. I couldn't go as a druida and certainly not as a warrior. We decided that I'd go as what I was, the son of a merchant looking to make his own fortune. There were plenty of the Keltoi doing that now, Draius told me, and the promise of commerce could get me into Rome itself. My new identity was as the son of the Bellovaci. The Bellovaci were a standoffish tribe, they had never fought Rome; they mostly just fought with and traded with the German tribes about them. With luck, I would not meet anyone who knew any of them. When Ludwa finished my clothes, she cut and oiled my hair in the Roman fashion, and dressed me in the style of Rome. My new name was Rufus.

I made a belt of gold coins and wore it around my waist under my garment, as I did with the sword of Brossix; strapped to my thigh. Draius gave me a horse. I only had one thing to give him; my mule. He said he liked it and would name it Marius. Draius had one more thing to say as I mounted. "The days of the druidae are over Vercassivellaunus; you are the last. Watch over the world." I rode south.

* * * * *

I traveled through the lands of our confederation and into the Transalpine with no trouble until I reached the land of the Allobroges; and that wasn't much trouble, I killed the man before it became so. The Provincia had been governed by Rome for a long time; the Allobroges were now Rome's lackeys, but they still liked to strut around and act like warriors. But they weren't anymore. I had stopped at an inn to spend the night. There was the usual mix of men that hung around those places, mostly travelers; but some get drunk and boisterous and although I tried to ignore those, one I couldn't. He was a slave trader now, for Rome and gold, and boasted of the women he had raped and killed and all I could think about was Ladia and Gesataia and women like them walking down that Roman road with Roman chains on them. When he went outside to piss, I followed him and slit his throat. No one seemed to miss him; I finished my supper and his companions kept talking and drinking.

* * * * *

The Greeks had long ago built the great port city of Massilia for their trade with Gaul but as Rome conquered more and more it built roads into Hispania and Gaul and their own port of Narbo. Goods came down our rivers and they were shipped to Rome. Ladia would have been brought here, and then on to Rome or somewhere on this sea the Romans called the Mare Nostrum. I took a room near the center of the city; I wanted to be seen as a prosperous Gaul who had taken the Roman way and to mingle with the men who dealt with Rome.

The next morning I went to the shops and bought fine Roman garb, and then to the baths. I was clean shaven and my hair was short and oiled and with my new clothes looked like what I wanted to be seen as. Now I had to learn to act the part. I needed to soften my appearance. It was impossible to erase the years of war and the winter in the mountains but I had to lose the demeanor of the wolf. I went to the wine shops and the inns and ate my meals and listened and watched. I kept to myself and paid attention to the conversations that civilized men have and learned what they ate and drank. I had learned Latin long ago with the druidae but sharpened my ear to the unfamiliar words until I felt comfortable enough to begin engaging in conversations. I had been there a week and was now seen as a familiar face in the crowd. I went to the shops and bought things, and practiced my Latin by haggling and discussing things with the shopkeepers. I started buying a few drinks in the wine shops and made a few acquaintances among the regulars. I learned the flow of the Roman world.

The man I wanted was called Marcus Traqcus. It didn't take long; asking around and buying a drink or two and the same name kept appearing. He was a Thracian taken years ago by Roman armies and made a slave, then a gladiator. He was never defeated and extremely popular with the Romans. When he bought his freedom, he went into business with some of the rich and now owned the monopoly of the slave trade from Gaul to

265

Rome. His agents were everywhere there was a Roman garrison. They bought the captured people from Roman soldiers and officers and brought them to Narbo where they were shipped to Rome.

Traqcus lived in Rome but came here several times a year to meet with his agents and clerks, but mostly just to show his power and remind people whom he represented. He was expected soon and usually stayed a week before he returned to Rome. When Traqcus came, it was easy to tell he was about. The activity picked up and people were scurrying about looking for the same thing I was; access to the man. I wanted more than that; I wanted to get inside of Rome. I made a point of being seen when he was about, kind of aimless but moving about and talking to people. Then on his fourth day in Narbo, I approached him in the square.

"Citizen Traqcus, my name is Rufus. I beg you forgive my straightforwardness but I've heard you have ships that go to Rome and I need go there. Is there a way?"

He was a big man, and almost brutal in appearance, but as I was soon to know not at all unaffable. He looked at me and greeted me openly enough; I could sense the wolf in him but he kept it deep inside and after taking my hand and exchanging pleasantries, he invited me to come to his offices in the next two days so I could conduct my business with his clerk. I guess this was a fairly common request. I paid for my passage the next morning, and two days later was on the sea for the first time in my life; on the way to Rome.

I didn't like this sea much, but at least I wasn't sick like some of the slaves. It had sails and some oars, but not many of them. I think they wanted room for what they carried to Rome. It was supposed to be three days travel to Rome but we stopped for a night and day on an island where Traqcus had a house and some other buildings in which he put the slaves.

He had talked to me some on our first day, asking about my tribe and where we lived and what I'd done, and all the things that men ask one another. He didn't say it, but I think he sensed what I was; or at least what I wasn't. I told him that we traded with some Germani tribes and fought others and I was looking for ways to enrich myself. He didn't say much about it.

At his island, he had the captives washed in the ocean and their long hair cut and gave them each a coarse tunic; and he invited me to come to his house for refreshment when the day was done. Traqcus treated me very civilly, almost cordially, though not quite. He showed me the weapons that he'd used in the gladiator battles and told me about them and about Rome. We talked of goods from the north that the Romans might want, and the products they would sell in return. Then I went back to the ship and slept, and a few hours later the men started loading the slaves aboard. We sailed for Rome.

* * * * *

I had never seen anything like that place and I hope that I never will again. I had a shop to go to and a man's name to ask for there. Draius knew people in most places and I had gold. First I would find a room. Traqcus had told me of an inn near the center of Rome where, he said; the men that mattered would stay and congregate.

The inn was mobbed with people, but when I told him in my improving Latin that Marcus Traqcus had recommended it to me they gave me a room. The common room was full too but I finally got a place on a bench with a lot of men who ignored me and I ate all I could convince the slave girl to bring me; the wine flowed easily though. I set out the next morning to find the man I needed. Draius had told me to go to a place they made jewelry on the south part of the Roman Forum and find a man named Jurix who owned the shop.

I've been cooped up in cities with sixty thousand warriors but this place was more crowded and probably more dangerous. I finally found the shop and Jurix and as I inquired about a torque, I casually mentioned that an old man who lived in a forest in Gaul had sent me to him. He very quietly told me where to meet him that night.

Jurix was not a dangerous man, but he knew people that were; I would need men with me, he said, men who were paid to protect the man that hired them. He came out of the shadows then; the man who would later save my life. His name was Winchus; he was a Keltoi of Hispania and he became my friend.

We walked the streets of Rome for two days; Winchus and I strolled and talked but kept to Latin mostly; always that when people were about us. There was a place, called the Carcer, where Romans who broke the law were taken. Below ground, there was an area where they kept prisoners, called the Tullianum. Below that, was an old cistern about fifteen feet across. When the great aqueducts began bringing water from the mountains, they plugged up the spring that fed this cistern and made it a place for special prisoners. It had no windows and was deep underground, and the only way in and out was a trap door in the top. Vercingetorix lived there with two buckets; one to bring food and water in and one to take his waste out. The trap door above was opened once a day.

Winchus and I stood outside that building. It was close to the government buildings and there were a lot of people going back and forth. I could sense Vercin and I think he probably sensed me too. I came back that night and we talked. Not the way people usually talk, but we talked. He asked me about Ladia and his boys and I told him only that I was looking for them. I told him of the Remi attack and that Draius sent me to Narbo and here. He asked me how I escaped Alesia and I told him of that and my winter on the mountain, and of Gerromir and Brossix and Commius and the rest, and of Gaul.

Later that night I was in a tavern, eating with Winchus. There was a man in there that I had seen before; he was looking at me, then he came over. "My name is Ugric and I belong to Marcus Traqcus; he sent me to tell you to come to his house tomorrow morning." Then the man left after laying a small paper before me that showed lines and arrows; a map to Traqcus's house I guess; anyway, I went there early.

Ugric met us at the door; he motioned Winchus to a bench and for me to follow him inside. Traqcus greeted me warmly, but I had that fear inside of me that I always have of the unknown, and of some known as well. He sat me at a table, unusual in itself, and poured me something from an amphorae that I hoped was wine and then he sat beside me.

"Who are you Rufus?" I didn't know how to answer him; I felt that he knew that what I had told him wasn't all, or even part of, the truth, so I sat. He sat and waited. Then he spoke.

"I've had men following you since you've been in Rome and your movements and actions aren't those of a young merchant looking for riches. Everything that goes on in Rome is my concern, Rufus. I'm not necessarily hostile toward you but I have to know your business here."

"I'm looking for a woman," I finally replied.

"Is that all? I can have Ugric take you to one right now. But surely the man with you can find you one." Traqcus laughed and I did myself; it did sound like a foolish statement. He kept staring at me though, waiting for more and serious again.

"She is special to me. A Gaul taken for a slave. It's been said that you would be the one who would have brought her here, or to somewhere."

Traqcus sat and stared at me; I felt no fear, or at least less fear now. "I have brought almost a million Gauls to Rome in the past five years; why is this one special?"

"Because she is dear to me and I promised to look after her." He could sense no lie from me but he also knew I wasn't telling everything. Nor would I; he sensed that too.

"So how can I help you? I assume you want my help or you wouldn't have approached me in Narbo. Do you want to look through my records? Would you go through lists of hundreds of thousands to find a name that half the women in Gaul would have?"

"I can start with the people taken since last summer. I'll find her there; or I will if you'll let me." I started within the hour. After another, I had found Ladia. You see, I didn't have to read the lists of names in the stacks of books he put before me. All I had to do was place my hand over the books, one by one, until I found the right one, then go through each page. When I touched the right one, I took that book to Traqcus and showed him the page. "She is this one."

I went to the Carcer again that night and told Vercin that I had found Ladia. I stood waiting but heard nothing. Then drops of water begin forming around my feet. I left.

PAT MIZELL

THIRTY YEARS LATER

I'm an old man now, and with my wife, the only ones left from those days. Vercingetorix has gone to his next life, Caesar is long dead, and all my friends have moved on. Now that Traqcus is gone, too, I can finally tell you the rest.

I went back to his house that next day and I was taken to a room that I hadn't seen on my previous visit. The walls appeared to be very thick and the only door was massive. Traqcus sat on a divan, there were others scattered around a table laid with fruit, bread, and all the delicious things Romans like, and of course, a wine. I had tasted it before at his home on the island.

"I will tell you a story, Rufus, about a man who was a king. He was a young king of an old land not too far from here, but the Romans came one day and took him and his people. He and they had fought savagely but Rome was too much for them and they were made slaves. This man was a fighter and noticed by some men who then made him a gladiator. He never lost a fight, but he grew to middle age by killing men; and he wanted more than that and less of that and as he aged he began to learn things that would help him. Some of these things came naturally to him but some he learned from others.

"Rome was conquering the world by now and thousands and thousands of people were brought here and made slaves. This man was unusual in that he had been a slave himself but had come from an elite background and so knew the ways of both. This man became a Roman; today he is one of the most powerful men in Rome. He isn't a Senator or a politician but he has connections with all of them and more than that with a few of them. You won't see this man's name on any of the grand buildings of Rome, or in any books, and the masses of Rome wouldn't know him, but the men that matter do. He serves few people, but to one he owes his life and everything else he has. This man holds life or death over you now. Tell me Rufus, why do you want Vercingetorix's wife?"

I had no choice. There are times in a man's life when he has no alternative but to take a stand, and be willing to die for it. I told him the truth, all of it this time. We sat there most of the day; I liked the man.

"I'll just continue to call you Rufus; I've a Roman tongue now but your name could twist even it." He smiled at me and for the first time in a long time, I smiled back at someone. My path was stated and the burden I carried was shared with another; for good or bad.

"There is not a way under all the gods of the sun that you can have Vercingetorix. He is the symbol of Caesar's greatness and all the gold in Gaul wouldn't buy him. He'll be the centerpiece in Caesar's Triumph. Other things are negotiable. You have something that my master would want.

The straight path of the life you think you're on will twist beyond anything you could ever imagine." Traqcus was on my path now, and I was on his. He served Caesar while I tried to kill him. He left for Caesar's villa in the Cisalpine and came back with a proposition for me; four days later.

"You can have her for one thing. That thing will never require you to harm your people. That thing will take you into no danger nor require you to answer to any man but me; and through me, my master.

We can take this conversation further into personal trust; you said you wanted to kill Romans? We are at a crossroads in Rome, Rufus. If Caesar is denied his due, Rome will erupt. Caesar has an army sitting in the Cisalpine. All that's between him and becoming an outlaw is one little river up there between his army and Italy. You have reached that point in this conversation with me. If we continue it you have crossed your river, and your die is cast.

*****

I left Rome with Ladia soon after that. There was one thing more I got. We left Rome on the same ship I had come there on. Ladia had been well cared for but she was very quiet and sad; she hadn't seen her children since the raid in the forest and she knew nothing about them. I would tell her what I knew, but not now. We were going home first.

On the way there we sailed by that little island where Traqcus had taken me once. There was a man standing on the beach as we passed. He was a tall blonde man and stared at us and we stared back at him. That was the last time I ever saw Vercingetorix.

Now I need to tell you what my end of the bargain was. I hope you trust me and know that it was the best I could do. Rome was collapsing from the inside in those days. This had started years before but now it was worse. The Republic which was supposed to serve all of Rome had become the property of the elite and Caesar meant to change that, or take it for himself. That was no matter to me. I just wanted to get Ladia out and keep Vercingetorix alive.

Caesar would have his way, or split Rome into pieces. The old families were fighting him but the citizens on the street adored him; and he had an army sitting on that little river north of Rome. The question was: would he have to use it to get his way? Then there was the question of would he use it if he had to? You know both those answers now, but then no one did, not even Caesar himself.

Caesar wanted my power; not in any physical sense, but he knew the power that a druida had. I gave it to him in return for Ladia and Vercingetorix. But that's a story for another day.

The End

PAT MIZELL

ABOUT THE AUTHOR

"I've always been fascinated by the acceptance of history as it is written. It seems to me that there are three sides to every story; the winner's, the loser's, and yours. I hope to give you two of those; you furnish the other."

Pat Mizell is in retreat at Browning Creek in north Mississippi where he lives with the voices of the past that want their stories told.

Printed in Great Britain
by Amazon